DANGER
ON THE
STAGE

By Steven K. Smith

MBZ PRESS

For more information, contact us at:

MyBoys3 Press, P.O. Box 2555, Midlothian, VA 23113

www.myboys3.com

First Printing

ISBN: 978-1-947881-38-9

In memory of my dear neighbor, Brian,
and to his wife, Sue, a true book lover

DANGER
ON THE
STAGE

PROLOGUE

They'd heard the sounds for the past mile. Eerie howls. First one, but then followed by more. Wolves in a pack, no doubt, tracking them through the forested hills. Stalking them from the cover of the trees. Now, shadows moved stealthily just beyond the pines, plotting their attack.

Daniel Boone's hunting party had been following the trail established by the Cherokee through the Holston and Clinch River valley. They hadn't glimpsed home for nearly six months, but now they moved steadily toward the gap in the Appalachian range and approached the westward passage through the mountains into Kentucky. The leaves were all nearly fallen, their deep oranges and reds turned a crinkled brown.

Their party's collection of furs for trade was growing from steady trapping, and so far, they'd avoided any major confrontation from either the Cherokee or wild beasts. They hadn't encountered wolves directly, but Boone had noted several nearby caves along the route that may have been lairs for the packs he knew were stalking them now. The hunting dogs had sensed them too, growing restless when they'd made camp the past two evenings.

The glow of the fire leapt into the darkness, blazing high from the extra logs heaped onto it in the hope of discouraging any attacks. Boone lifted a torch and moved three cautious steps beyond the circle of their bedrolls, peering into the surrounding hills that were wrapped in the darkness of the night. He gripped the cold steel barrel of his rifle. He'd spent many nights under the stars, amongst the wild. More than he could remember. And he knew it was only a matter of time until the wolves moved in.

CHAPTER ONE

S am stared at his watch for the hundredth time and sighed.

"Stop looking. It won't help," Caitlin said, seated next to him in the middle row of the car.

"I know, but I don't want to be late."

"Relax, will you?" said Derek from the back. "You're almost as bad as Grandma."

Sam frowned. Their grandma thought that if you weren't at least twenty minutes early to everything, you were late. That was clearly too extreme, but he appreciated where she was coming from. Early was definitely better than late, and if it meant wasting a little time, so be it. "I am not. I just don't want to miss our chance to meet Jake."

"You mean Mr. Greensboro?" said Caitlin.

"I'll give you five bucks if you call him Jake to his face," said Derek, laughing.

"We'll be there shortly," Mrs. Murphy assured them from the front seat. "And if we miss the chance to meet him before the show, I'm sure we can see Mr. Greensboro after."

Derek tapped Sam's shoulder. "Plus, they'll probably have previews before the main show starts."

"It's a play," said Sam, "not a movie. I don't think they have previews."

"Well, then we'll just be fashionably late. You know, so everyone has to turn around and notice us."

Sam shook his head. That was exactly what he didn't want to happen. "Of course you'd like that. It's your fault we're in this situation in the first place."

His brother shrugged. "Hey, I said I was sorry, okay? How was I supposed to know you were waiting on the other side of the rest stop building? Maybe if you'd looked for me…"

"Maybe if we'd left you there…" Sam muttered under his breath. Derek had gotten lost in the parking lot after a bathroom break on the way down Interstate 81, driving from Richmond to Abingdon.

Caitlin chuckled next to him. "You're really excited to see him, aren't you?"

"No," Sam answered. "Well, yeah, I guess. I also just hate being late."

Derek laughed again behind them. "I think Sam has a man-crush on Mr. Greensboro."

Sam shot his brother a nasty look. Derek being a jerk was nothing new, but this was a special opportunity for all of them. Jacob Greensboro was one of Sam's favorite actors. He played the hero from Sam's favorite detective movie franchise.

Jake didn't normally perform live, but it turned out that he got his start in acting twenty years ago on the Abingdon stage. In an even bigger coincidence, Caitlin's aunt Ginny was the current artistic director of the Barter Theatre in Abingdon. When Caitlin's mom had invited Sam and Derek to join their family for opening night, it was too good of an offer to turn down. Sam had tried to convince Mrs. Murphy that everything would be much more fun without his older brother, but she had just laughed. She'd said they had two rooms booked at the hotel already, so this way the boys could stay in one room, and Caitlin could stay in the second with her parents. Sam guessed that kind of made sense, although if it hadn't been for the prospect of meeting Jacob Greensboro, he wasn't sure whether staying in a hotel room alone with Derek would have been worth it.

He stared out the window, watching the trees fly by along the highway. It was a long drive from Richmond all the way to Abingdon. Caitlin had said, even after driving for hours, they were still in southwest Virginia. Sam had had to look at a map before he'd believed her, but it was true. A thin sliver of land in the southwest part of the state was sandwiched between West Virginia and Kentucky to the north and North Carolina and Tennessee to the south.

Sam ducked as Caitlin nearly clocked him in the head

as she pulled her guitar into the seat next to him. She'd been taking lessons for the past year and was now convinced that she was going to become the next country music star. Sam had to admit, she was pretty good after such a short amount of time, but he was reserving judgment about whether she was ready to become the next American Idol.

"I wish I could hold down these bar chords better," Caitlin moaned as she finger-picked quietly.

"Wouldn't it be more fun to play an electric guitar?" asked Derek.

Caitlin played a short melody she'd been working on for half the car ride and shook her head. "I like the acoustic sound better. Plus, it's easier." She glanced back at Derek. "It would be hard to play if I had to have an amplifier with me everywhere."

Derek groaned and slid back in the seat, covering his ears. "My point exactly."

Mr. Murphy turned off the highway, driving slower until they reached a red traffic light on Main Street. Caitlin leaned in front of Sam to see out his window. "Is that The Martha?"

"I believe it is," her mom answered.

Mr. Murphy tapped on the steering wheel, waiting for the light to change. "Which means the Barter Theatre should be just ahead on the other side of the road."

"Can't we stop and throw our things in the room first?" Derek asked, as they slowly passed a black iron railing that separated a front lawn from the street. A sign in the grass read: *The Martha. Hotel and Spa.*

"No!" Sam yelled, his voice louder than he'd intended. Everyone turned and raised their eyebrows at him. "I mean, we need to hurry so we can meet Jake, remember?" he quickly added.

"That car's pulling out," Mrs. Murphy called, pointing to an open spot.

When the light turned green, Mr. Murphy zipped forward and smoothly parallel parked along the curb.

"Perfect! Nice job, Daddy," said Caitlin.

Sam glanced up at the building on the other side of the fence. The Martha sounded like a weird name for a hotel, but he remembered Caitlin telling him that its full name was The Martha Washington Inn. Apparently, it was pretty old. She said it also used to be a women's college during the Civil War. The building's greenish-colored roof was lined with curved dormer windows above a long front porch. A pair of three-story wings surrounded the main structure, which had tall, white columns like on an old bank building.

"Woah, look at that." Derek pointed to the car parked in front of them. It was a silver Porsche with a personalized plate that read "ENCORE."

Sam caught his breath. "Do you think that's Jake's car?" He jumped out and ran up the sidewalk to get a better look. The sparkling silver paint job certainly made it look like a movie star's car.

Caitlin pointed back at the hotel. "Maybe he's staying here, too."

Sam's jaw dropped. "Really?"

"It's quite possible," said Mr. Murphy. "We're right across from the theater, and it's probably the nicest place in town. Certainly the most historic."

"Wow…" Sam marveled. "Maybe we'll see him at breakfast."

Caitlin grabbed Sam's arm and tugged him up the sidewalk. "We won't see him at all if we don't hurry up. Remember how much you wanted to get to the theater on time?"

Sam nodded and quickly followed along. "Oh yeah. The show. I almost forgot."

Derek shook his head. "You're such a fangirl."

"Am not."

Caitlin giggled. "You kind of are."

CHAPTER TWO

They crossed at the corner and walked toward a brick building with a crowd of people gathered in front along the sidewalk. Even from a distance, it was easy to see the bright-colored flags lining the edges of the peaked roof. A single, much bigger flag that billowed out over the sidewalk read "Barter Theatre." The marque sign proclaimed that it was "The State Theatre of Virginia."

"Why is it called the Barter?" asked Sam. "Was that somebody's name?"

"Believe it or not, the theater opened during the Depression," answered Mrs. Murphy. "Families in this area traded crops and produce from their farms, sometimes even livestock, in order to attend the shows."

"They bartered!" exclaimed Caitlin.

Mrs. Murphy smiled. "Exactly. I read it could get pretty noisy. Sometimes the performers had to talk over the ruckus from the animals that were being stored in the space that's now the lobby."

Sam tilted his head. "Is that really true?"

Mrs. Murphy laughed and pointed to a large box outside the door. "I wouldn't lead you wrong, Sam. In fact, at some points throughout the year, they still collect canned goods for the needy in return for tickets because of that old tradition."

"Why don't I slip inside to grab the tickets?" said Mr. Murphy. "Ginny said she'd leave them for us at the box office." He marched up the steps and through the doorway as the rest of them waited outside.

Derek looked confused. "You'd think they'd at least know how to spell theater. They put the 'r' before the 'e.' How embarrassing."

Caitlin chuckled. "It's spelled both ways. Theatre with an 're' is the British way."

"Well, that's confusing," muttered Derek.

Sam stared up at another large sign. *Now Playing: The Adventures of Little Red Riding Hood. With Special Guest, Jacob Greensboro.* He didn't know why a big action star like Jake would choose to perform in a silly kids' story like Little Red Riding Hood. But getting to see Jake in person was a treat, no matter what show it was.

"Sam, you coming in, or are you just going to stare at the sign all night?" Derek called from the steps. He pointed at Mr. Murphy inside the doorway with paper tickets in his hand.

Sam's stomach did a quick somersault at the prospect

of being able to get backstage and meet Jake before the show began. "Coming!"

Derek studied his glossy paper ticket. "Where are our seats? Are we in the front row?"

"We're actually up in the balcony," answered Mrs. Murphy. "I think it was the best Ginny could do for five tickets for opening night at late notice."

Derek shrugged. "The balcony's cool."

Caitlin's eyes sparkled. "I can't believe we get to see opening night!"

Sam stood next to the refreshment station and a wall filled with mugs and Christmas ornaments. He eyed the packed lobby anxiously, as if Jacob Greensboro might bump into him at any moment. The famous actor was close to Sam's dad's age, so Sam didn't know exactly what he'd say to the man, but he figured he'd come up with something.

Caitlin must have noticed his expression and chuckled. "He's probably getting ready backstage, silly."

Sam took a long breath and tried to relax. He turned casually to Mrs. Murphy. "I thought we might get to see him beforehand?"

"Ginny said maybe if time allowed. It just depends on whether we can see her before the—wait, there she is now!" She waved her hand above the crowd. "Ginny! Over here!"

A woman in a long, black velvet dress pushed through the crowd with a wide smile. She looked a lot like Caitlin's mom.

"You made it!" Ginny wrapped Mrs. Murphy in a tight hug and then bounced up to see the rest of them. "Oh, my goodness! Caitlin, what a young woman you've become!" She repeated the dive-bomb hug on Caitlin and Mr. Murphy. "Thanks for coming, y'all."

"Are you kidding? We wouldn't miss it." Caitlin introduced Sam and Derek and then nodded toward the door Ginny had come out of. "Think we might say a quick hi to Mr. Greensboro?"

Ginny peeked at her watch and gave a mischievous nod as she lowered her voice. "Just for a second. It is almost show time, and well, you know how these artists are with their process. We don't want to mess with his performance." She glanced at Caitlin's parents. "Maybe I can just take the kids this time, if you two don't mind. It's tight quarters back there."

"No problem," said Mr. Murphy. "We'll see you guys in the balcony. Your seat numbers are marked on your tickets."

Caitlin, Sam, and Derek followed Ginny in a thin line through the crowd. They passed the box office and a wall lined with dozens of old photos and went through a door that led to a dimmed hallway. The backstage area they'd entered was painted black from floor to ceiling. Scenery, props, equipment, and cast and crew were everywhere. Set pieces stood on wheels, some hung on tracks up near the ceiling, and others were secured by ropes weighted down by sandbags or tied off along the wall. A dark red curtain ran along the stage edge, held up at the ceiling on a runner attached to metal scaffolding full of light cans, ropes, and other equipment.

Ginny turned behind a wall and went down a stairway into a short hallway with a row of doors. "It's been a madhouse here lately. In the middle of rehearsals, a pipe burst and flooded several offices. I had to temporarily move my desk into the Wardrobe Room of all places." Ginny stopped in front of a door with a star on it and threw her hands in the air. "It's pure chaos!"

Caitlin nudged Sam excitedly as her aunt knocked on the door. "It's his dressing room!"

Suddenly Sam wasn't so sure if this was such a great idea after all. Seeing someone on TV or a movie screen was a lot different to standing face-to-face. The only famous people he'd actually met in person were ballplayers signing autographs at Yankee Stadium during batting practice. But then he'd just been one of a dozen nameless hands reaching out along the outfield wall with programs and pens. And while a couple players had made brief eye contact and smiled, they hadn't spoken.

"Come in," a deep voice answered from behind the door.

Ginny cracked the door open and stuck in her head. "Jake, I'm so sorry to bother you, but those young fans I mentioned to you were hoping to say hello. Would you mind?"

Sam didn't hear an answer, but the door opened wide and Derek shoved him forward into the dressing room. Sam tried to stop his brother from pushing him, but before he knew it, he stood at the front of their small group. He glanced up as someone stood up from a makeup table with bright lights outlining the mirror.

The figure suddenly lunged forward at Sam. A wild, hairy face was only inches from his, a wide mouth with glistening teeth drawing Sam's attention most. "The better to *meet* you with!" a voice roared.

Sam screamed in an embarrassingly high pitch and jumped back into Derek and Caitlin, stumbling and ending up on the floor. Everyone cracked up as Sam quickly realized what had happened. Jacob Greensboro was already in his wolf costume for the play.

"That was great!" Derek laughed and pushed Sam back to his feet. "I think you gave my little brother a heart attack. Can you do it again?"

"I'm sorry, I couldn't resist," the wolf, or Jacob Greensboro, said quickly. He reached out and patted Sam's arm with a hairy paw. "Are you okay, young man?"

Sam pushed his brother away and stood tall. This was not how he'd imagined things going. "I'm fine, thank you. Nice to meet you."

"Sam's one of your biggest fans," said Caitlin.

Mr. Greensboro gave another wide, saber-toothed grin. "Well, I'm glad you came for opening night. I hope I don't disappoint. It's great to be back in this old theater after all these years. It's where I got my start, you know."

A curly-haired woman leaned her head through the doorway. "Curtain's up in five minutes."

"Well, I'm afraid that's my cue," said Jacob. "Maybe we can see each other again after the show."

"Oh, and Mr. Greensboro—" The curly-haired woman held out an envelope. "This just came for you. It's marked urgent."

The wolf's big, bushy eyebrows bounced at the news. "Ah, fan mail. It never ends." He held up his costumed hands, outfitted in some sort of gloves with fake claws. "Can't really open it with these dandies." He leaned toward Sam. "Be a help and open it for me, will you? I always savor a few words of encouragement before the curtain rises."

Sam felt his heart thump in his chest as he took the envelope. Not only was he in Jacob Greensboro's dressing room, but he was about to open his fan mail! Sam peeled at the glued envelope closure, but it didn't open cleanly. The paper started ripping into small pieces, coming off in bits. He felt his face reddening. "Sorry, I always have trouble with these."

Derek shook his head and stifled a laugh. "Geez, Sam. Why don't you just put it through the shredder?"

Sam tried to ignore his brother and finally pulled a single, folded sheet from the mangled envelope. He held it out to Jake. "Here you go."

Greensboro didn't take the paper. He turned back to the mirror and admired his hairy reflection. "Read it to me, will you?"

Sam glanced at Caitlin excitedly. She motioned he should keep going, so he unfolded the paper. It was a letter. But as Sam stared down at the writing, it quickly felt like someone had dropped a cinderblock in his stomach.

"Um…" His eyes raced over the words scrawled in a messy ink across the middle of the page. This was all wrong. He glanced up at Jake and then the others. "I don't think it's what you were expecting."

This wasn't fan mail. It was a death threat!

Jake sighed. "It's not inappropriate photos, is it? I'm sorry, I don't know why some people think—" He turned and studied the words on the paper, then looked down at the floor. "Oh, dear. Not again."

Ginny stepped up and took the letter from Sam's hands. "If you take the stage tonight, it will be your last performance. Are you willing to barter your life?" She gasped and looked up. "Oh my goodness."

"Woah," said Derek. "That's serious."

"Who would write something like that?" cried Caitlin.

Ginny shook her head. "I don't know, but…" She paused, rubbing her temples. She looked over at them, and then looked back at the actor. "We'll have to cancel the show. We can't let something violent happen."

Jake held up his menacing paw. "No! We're not canceling. Sadly, I've received messages like this before. It's just some confused, overzealous fan seeking attention. We can't let it ruin the performance."

Sam looked at the paper and then up at the wolf. "Are you sure? It sounds pretty serious."

"Absolutely." The actor motioned to the door. "Besides, there's no time. We're about to start. The show must go on!"

"Jake..." Ginny didn't look so sure. She glanced at the clock and then motioned them all back into the hall. "I think you kids better get up to your seats."

"You're going to let him go on?" asked Caitlin.

"But what about the letter?" said Sam.

Ginny's face was pale. "I don't know, but Mr. Greensboro is much more adept at dealing with celebrity than I am. If he says it's okay, maybe we'll just report it to the police after the show."

Sam didn't know if that was the greatest idea, but he was already being shuttled out to the hallway and up the backstage stairs.

"Come on," urged Caitlin. "The show is going to start soon, and we have to get up to the balcony."

CHAPTER THREE

Sam's mind was whirling as they crossed the lobby to the balcony level staircase. A woman with a hand-held xylophone tapped out a series of notes near the entrance. The show was about to begin.

"Let's not say anything to my parents about the letter," whispered Caitlin. "There's nothing they can do about it now, and I want them to enjoy the show." The lights were just dimming as they presented their tickets to the attendant in the balcony. She used a tiny flashlight to lead them forward, shining her light on the markers along the aisle. She stopped at the first row and pointed toward three empty middle seats next to Mr. and Mrs. Murphy.

"Excuse us," Caitlin whispered to the other guests in their row, stepping toward her parents in the narrow section in front of the seats.

Sam followed behind her slowly, trying not to bang

into anyone's shins, but it was a tight fit. An old lady with a furry wrap over her shoulders glared at him when he stepped on her toes. "Sorry." He grimaced and sank into the seat beside Caitlin.

"Just wait till you see the wolf," Derek proclaimed as he sat down. "We just met him backstage."

The old lady leaned forward and shushed him.

"Sorry," Derek whispered back, "but we're VIPs."

Sam tried to force the threatening letter from his mind as he gazed down at the theater in front of him. He was surprised to feel close to the stage, even from the balcony. It wasn't an enormous theater, unlike the Broadway show he'd been to with his parents in New York City just before they'd moved to Virginia. This one was smaller and more intimate, with a few hundred seats rather than a few thousand.

The seats were covered in the same velvety red fabric as the theater walls. Glass chandeliers glowed dimly across the ceiling, and several seats jutted out in both front corners of the balcony, like special luxury boxes at a basketball arena.

The murmurs from the crowd quickly quieted as a figure walked in front of the curtain at the edge of the stage.

"Good evening!" Ginny proclaimed, smiling widely as the spotlight focused down on her. "Welcome to the Barter Theatre. We're so appreciative that you have joined us for a very special production of *Red Riding Hood*."

Caitlin nudged Sam with her elbow. There was no

sign of the nervousness Ginny had shown in the dressing room. Caitlin had said that her aunt had spent most of her life working and performing in the theater. Maybe once you stepped out on the stage, everything else faded away.

"This opening night is special for several reasons," Ginny continued. "We're celebrating our wonderful founder, Robert Porterfield, who established the Barter back in 1933 amid the Great Depression. He believed that no matter where folks lived, they deserved to hear great stories told well. He famously advertised the ability for locals to exchange their goods for tickets as 'Ham for *Hamlet*,' and he said that 'With vegetables you cannot sell, you can buy a good laugh.' Today our repertory theater continues as a pillar of the arts in southwestern Virginia and is one of the nation's longest running professional theater companies.

"Tonight is the anniversary of Robert Porterfield's death in 1971, but we think he'd be proud of *Red Riding Hood*, selected in part because of Abingdon's original name of Wolf Hills, coined by Daniel Boone back in 1760 when wolves attacked his hunting expedition. As far as we know, there were no girls dressed in red cloaks around that night on the frontier, but the presence of wolves seemed an appropriate connection for the classic tale made famous by Charles Perrault and the Brothers Grimm."

Sam had heard of the famous explorer and frontiersman, Daniel Boone. Did he wear a coonskin cap, or was that Davy Crockett? Either way, he didn't realize there was a connection between him and Abingdon, although the name Wolf Hills didn't exactly sound like a place to settle down. So he could understand why they had changed it.

"Last, but most certainly not least, we are so very privileged to welcome the return of a cherished Barter alumnus, someone who acted in productions of *Midsummer Night's Dream*, *Our Town*, and *Macbeth* back in his days as a fresh-faced young man. He has gone on to star in countless roles in television and cinema, most notably his famous role as the fearless detective, Clint Patterson. I just ran into him backstage in full costume and makeup, and I can attest that what you are about to see from him is truly terrifying. I mean, spectacular."

The crowd laughed heartily.

"See, I'm not the only one," Sam muttered to Derek.

"Starring in the role of the wolf this evening is the wonderful Jacob Greensboro!"

Cheers and applause filled the room. Several people even rose from their seats as they clapped. Maybe Sam wasn't the only super fan who had come to watch Jake perform.

Ginny gestured toward the curtain. "We are so glad you've joined us tonight as the Barter Theatre presents, *Red Riding Hood*!"

Again, the crowd applauded, as Ginny bowed and slipped back into the darkness. Sam thought she'd done a good job of carrying on as usual despite the threat of danger. He took a long breath and trained his attention down to the stage as the lights came up. The velvety curtain parted and slid toward the wings. The scenery looked much more impressive than when he'd glimpsed it from backstage. Images of a thick forest, bushes, and rocks along a path all sparkled under the stage lights.

The spotlight focused on a young woman leaning against a rock on the side of the path. As expected, she wore a deep red cloak and clutched an oversized picnic basket. While she explained how her mother had sent her through the forest to deliver food to her sick grand-mother, a pair of menacing eyes glowed in the shadows.

Almost immediately, Sam's hesitation about watching a silly story and his worries over the letter disappeared. Maybe it was the lighting, the set design, or just the way the actors talked, but it felt like he was reading a good book. He had forgotten how theater could temporarily transport you into a different time and place, letting you experience someone else's life in a way that you couldn't or wouldn't want to do on your own. He felt like he was there in the forest, listening to the poor girl rattle on about her trip to Grandma's house, unaware that a wolf stalked her nearby.

When the glowing eyes finally stepped out into the spotlight, hoots and cheers erupted from the audience. But a shiver shot down Sam's spine at the memory of Jake surprising him in the dressing room. Nonetheless, he settled into his seat as the wolf sneakily inquired about the girl's destination.

As the show progressed, Sam wondered how such a dark plot could exist in a well-known fairy tale. Who in their right mind would send their daughter alone into the wolf-filled woods with a picnic basket? By the end of the first act, the beast had convinced Red Riding Hood to stop and pick some flowers. Meanwhile, he raced ahead to Grandma's house, swallowed the unfortunate woman whole, and waited in disguise in her bed for poor Red Riding Hood's arrival.

As the house lights came up between acts, Sam leaned toward Caitlin. "Who the heck came up with this story?"

"Shh." She giggled and moved forward in her seat. "It's a classic."

Sam shook his head. "A classic horror story, maybe."

The second act opened with Red Riding Hood greeting her unusually hairy grandma. As the conversation continued, she gradually suspected that something was seriously wrong. Sam thought back to Jake's words in the dressing room as Red Riding Hood exclaimed her famous lines about "what a deep voice, big eyes and hands you have."

Derek nudged him excitedly. "This is the part I've been waiting for."

Maybe it was because of the scare backstage, but despite the scene reaching its climax on the stage, Sam's attention turned to the audience. Who could have sent that letter? Was it a hoax, or was someone really planning something sinister if Jake performed in the show? Everyone around Sam seemed fully absorbed in the story, despite knowing that the innocent girl was about to be attacked by a vicious wolf.

Sam's eyes landed on the far side of the balcony. A man stepped slowly down the aisle toward the special corner box seats. Even in the near-darkness, his white, three-piece suit practically glowed. When the man reached the edge of the balcony, he turned and seemed to look directly at Sam. He smiled, not in a creepy way, but more like he was just being friendly. He gave a quick wave across the balcony, but no one else seemed to notice. They were all paying rapt attention to the show down below. Was Sam the only one who saw him? What was he doing?

A commotion sounded from down on the stage as Red Riding Hood exclaimed what big teeth her grandma had. Caitlin reached over and squeezed Sam's arm at what was about to follow. Right on cue, the wolf roared and leaped from the bed. He threw off his grandma night-gown, towering over the trembling girl in the middle of the stage. "The better to *eat* you with!"

That was when Red Riding Hood let out the loudest, most blood-curdling scream Sam had ever heard. The entire audience seemed to jump in their seats. Even Derek almost fell out of his chair. Caitlin's fingernails dug into the skin on Sam's wrist so hard he thought she might draw blood.

But then everything went wrong.

Sam glanced back at the man in the white suit. He was pointing at the stage.

When Red Riding Hood screamed a second time, a blur swung down from the ceiling and past the curtain. It looked like a sandbag tied to one of the ropes that held the set pieces in place. It flew straight past the wolf and Red Riding Hood and smashed into the fake wall of Grandma's bedroom. Was it part of the show, or was something wrong?

Sam peered at the bedroom set. The tall, wooden structure had been knocked cockeyed. He thought for a moment it might stand firm, but then it wobbled and tilted forward, falling straight at the two lead actors in the middle of the stage.

Without thinking, Sam leapt from his seat. "Watch out!" he shouted down to the stage.

In a normal place and time, Caitlin would have grabbed his arm and pulled him back to his seat, Derek would have laughed, and the old lady with stepped-on toes would have leaned across and shushed him.

But there was no time for any of that.

Sam sensed a brief gasp from the audience. For an instant, even Jake seemed to break character, his attention turning to the noise from the balcony while his arms were raised above the girl.

But then the scenery wall crashed down. Somehow, Red Riding Hood stepped back just far enough to dodge the set whooshing past her nose. Jake wasn't so swift. He caught the full weight of the wooden wall. It slammed down on him with a thud.

CHAPTER FOUR

I t took a moment for the audience to process what had happened. Even in the chaos, some apparently thought it was still part of the show. A smattering of applause sounded from the left. But then the music stopped. The spotlight froze off-center, casting the actors and the rubble of the set in uneven shadows. Sam leaned forward and watched stagehands run in from the wings. They talked loudly and worked together to pull at the set pieces on top of Jake.

Sam didn't know if the falling wall had knocked Jake out cold, or if it was his voice that could be heard moaning loudly. The buzz in the audience quickly turned from surprise to alarm. Then the red curtains drew in from the sides, blocking the view of the stage. Sam glanced back to the front corner of the balcony. What had the man in the white suit been doing right before the commotion? Had he pointed at the ceiling above the stage?

Derek leaned over, wide-eyed. "That was intense. I totally forgot that part of the story. Is this another intermission?"

"That wasn't part of the play," said Caitlin. "Something's wrong."

"It's just like the letter said!"

Caitlin studied Sam's expression curiously. "Why did you stand up and yell?"

"I don't know." He tried to replay the scene in his head. "Did you see that guy?"

"The wolf?" asked Caitlin.

"That shock backstage must have affected you even more than I thought." said Derek. "That was Jacob Greensboro. We met him before the show when he scared the stuffing out of you…"

"No, not Jake." Sam shook his head impatiently. "I mean the guy in the white suit. He was at the edge of the balcony…"

The house lights slowly rose as Ginny spoke from the stage. "Ladies and gentlemen, can I please have your attention?" This time, her expression was grim. "I'm sorry, but as you may have seen, we've had an accident on the stage. I need you to all keep your seats until we assess the situation."

"That's not good," said Derek.

"Do you think Jake's hurt?" asked Sam.

Derek nodded. "That board really socked him good.

All that wood must weigh a couple hundred pounds, at least."

Caitlin stood and peered at the seats below. "Do you really think this has to do with the letter?"

"Either that, or it's a mighty big coincidence," said Derek.

The house lights were bright now, and a restless energy flowed through the audience. Someone poked their head between the curtains and whispered something to Ginny. She squinted at the crowd, shielding her eyes from the lights with her hand. "Is anyone a doctor?" she called with urgency in her voice. A man quickly stepped up onto the stage and out of sight.

Sam watched Ginny huddle with someone else at the right edge of the stage, her hands on her hips. She nodded and walked slowly back to the center of the stage before she faced the audience. "Ladies and gentlemen, I'm afraid we're unable to continue tonight's performance. Please follow the ushers as they direct you out of the theater in a calm and orderly fashion. Thank you for your cooperation."

"What do you think will happen to Jake?" asked Sam. With the curtain drawn, it was impossible to know what was taking place on stage.

"I have no idea," Mrs. Murphy answered. "But I think we need to leave."

"Let's all stay together." Mr. Murphy directed them toward the balcony exit.

It wasn't exactly chaos, but the lobby was abuzz when

they reached the bottom of the stairs. Patrons streamed noisily out onto the sidewalk.

"It was the letter," Sam whispered. "It had to be."

"Let's wait here," Mrs. Murphy called to them. "I want to speak with Ginny and see if there's anything we can do to help." She sighed and bit her lip. "I just feel terrible for her."

"I need you folks to continue exiting the lobby, please." An usher was motioning them toward the street. "We need to clear the theater for the evening."

"Whatever happened to 'the show must go on,' and all that stuff?" Derek called.

The man shook his head. "The show won't be resuming tonight."

"We're related to Ginny Moss," Mr. Murphy explained. "We were hoping to speak to her before we left."

The usher shook his head. "Everyone needs to leave."

"We're VIPs," Derek boasted.

Sam wondered if they were going to argue, but then Ginny emerged from the interior door. She looked exhausted, but she waved when she saw them across the lobby. She walked over and patted the usher's shoulder. "It's okay, George. They're with me. I'll take care of seeing them out."

The man looked disappointed that his authority had been undermined, but he nodded and stepped away quietly.

Derek shot the man a smirk and mouthed the letters "VIP."

Caitlin smacked his arm as she turned to her aunt. "What's happening, Aunt Ginny?"

Sam thought the woman looked like she'd aged ten years in the last hour. She nodded toward the theater. "Let's duck back in there where it's quieter."

She led them down the right aisle to the edge of the stage. Everything looked so different with vacant rows of seats staring back at them. The curtain had reopened, but the stage was now bare. The wooden bedroom piece that had fallen leaned against the back wall. There was no sign of Jake or the actress playing Red Riding Hood.

Sam shielded his eyes from the stage lights and peered up into the scaffolding. He spotted several long ropes, some still secured to set pieces, and some that dangled to the floor. A couple were connected to sandbags, which he knew worked as counterbalances to hold the sets. Had one just come loose, or did it have help?

He turned around and glanced up at the corner box at the edge of the balcony. There was no sign of the odd man in the white suit. Had that really happened, or was it just Sam's imagination?

"What a night," Ginny sighed, a tear slipping down her cheek.

Mrs. Murphy pulled her sister into a hug. "I'm so sorry, Ginny. What happened?"

Ginny shook her head solemnly. "I can't explain it, really. I've never seen anything like it in all my years in the theater. One moment everything was flowing perfectly, the next, sets were crashing down."

"Is Jake okay?" asked Caitlin.

"I hope so." Ginny stared backstage into the wing. "The ambulance took him out on a stretcher. The wall landed hard on his leg, and I fear he may have a concussion. But at least he was conscious."

"My goodness," said Mrs. Murphy.

"It really clocked him, huh?" exclaimed Derek.

"I saw the sandbag swing down from the ceiling before it knocked into the set," blurted Sam. "I don't know if it was the man in the white suit or not—it all happened so fast."

Ginny looked over at him. "What man, Sam?"

The door to the lobby opened with a bang, and a deep voice called across the room. Ginny cringed and muttered something under her breath. They turned and saw a stout and serious-looking man in a dark suit with a thick gray mustache walking down the aisle toward the stage. He reminded Sam of the man from the Monopoly game. Trailing two steps behind was a police officer, but even in a few seconds, it was easy to tell which of the men held the power.

"Who's that?" Sam asked.

Ginny's posture straightened. "That's Bernard Hostetter. He's our financial backer for this production."

Derek's eyes widened. "The money man."

"He looks serious," Caitlin said.

"He always looks serious," Ginny replied. "You'll have to excuse me."

"Are you in trouble?" asked Sam.

Ginny tried to fake a smile. "Shutting down a premier mid-show will never land well. And Bernard is not a man who likes to lose his investments. It's time to face the music. This could take a while. Hopefully, I'll connect with you tomorrow."

"Why don't we all head over to The Martha." Mr. Murphy pointed to the other aisle, so they could leave without colliding with the other men. Hostetter's booming voice exploded like a cannon as they walked to the lobby.

Caitlin stopped and glanced back toward the stage. "Can't we do something to help her?"

Mrs. Murphy reached out and squeezed Caitlin's shoulder. "Ginny's a big girl. She knows how to handle herself. Did I ever tell you about the time when she had to stand up against the entire senior class in the cafeteria?"

Caitlin rolled her eyes. "Only about a hundred times, Mom."

Mrs. Murphy chuckled. "Well then, you know she'll be fine."

"What happened in the cafeteria?" asked Derek. "Did she start a food fight?"

Caitlin held up her hand before her mom could answer. "I could tell this story with my eyes closed. Mom was a freshman in high school and she'd tried to bleach her hair, but instead of lightening it, it turned green. The biggest, meanest guy on the football team started calling Mom 'turnip top' every time he saw her, but after a few days of that, Aunt Ginny walked over and walloped the guy."

The boys looked at Mrs. Murphy in amazement. "She nailed him?"

"Right in the jaw."

"Did she get in trouble?" asked Sam.

Mrs. Murphy grinned. "She had to stay home for a couple of days according to school policy. Not that punching someone is ever okay, but it was nice that she stood up for her little sister."

"Wow," marveled Derek. "She's a tough cookie." He tussled Sam's hair with his fingers. "Maybe I can stand up for you like that sometime, Sam."

"Right." Sam rolled his eyes. "You'd probably run for the hills if anyone was causing trouble."

"What? I would not. You know I always help you out. You just never do anything that needs bravery like that."

Sam shook his head. "I live with you every day. Trust me, that takes a lot of bravery."

Mr. Murphy laughed heartily as he opened the door to the sidewalk. "Come on. Let's go get checked in to our hotel."

CHAPTER FIVE

Wh+en they left the theater, a few groups still lingered in front of the Barter, but most of the audience had dispersed to their cars or had wandered further along Main Street. The boys and Caitlin's family crossed the road between a row of lights that formed an illuminated crosswalk and walked back to the Murphys' car to retrieve their luggage. Caitlin's oversized guitar case banged into Derek's shoulder as she pulled it from the hatch.

"Why don't you just leave that in the car?" asked Derek.

"How would I play it if it's in the car, silly?"

"Exactly."

She frowned. "That's the second time you've said something like that. It's not nice."

"Welcome to my world," muttered Sam.

Mr. Murphy moved the car to The Martha's parking

lot while everyone else stepped onto the wide covered porch that ran the length of the main building. Even after dark, several people sat in the white rocking chairs or wicker patio furniture enjoying the warm evening.

A metal plaque mounted to the brick beside the main door said the hotel was on the National Register of Historic Places. "Wow," exclaimed Sam. "Everything in this town is old."

Caitlin moved next to him and read another sign above the plaque. "This house was built by General Francis Preston and his wife, Sarah Buchanan Campbell Preston, 1830-1832. That's sweet."

Derek stepped behind them with his duffel slung over his shoulder. "That's a long name. It's like the lady from Mount Vernon."

"It *is* called the Martha Washington Inn, genius." Sometimes Sam thought his brother really liked to state the obvious.

"No, not her, the other lady with the really long name. The one that saved the mansion."

Caitlin's face flashed with recognition. "Oh, you mean Ann Pamela Cunningham, the founder of the Mount Vernon Ladies Association?"

Derek nodded. "Yeah, that one."

Sam raised his eyebrows. "How'd you remember her?"

Derek grinned. "I have a memory like an elephant, Sam. You need to be careful. You never know what I might remember. I just forget I can do it sometimes." He cracked up at his own joke and pushed past them into the lobby of the inn.

Mrs. Murphy laughed. "I forgot what a character he can be."

Sam shook his head. "You have no idea."

The lobby looked more like the entrance to a spacious home than a hotel. A staircase rose in front of them, and to the left was a sitting room with couches, tables, and a fireplace. A crystal chandelier hung from the ceiling and a dark wood check-in desk filled the back wall beneath a wide mirror.

"Pretty fancy," said Derek.

"May I help you?" A man in his twenties walked in from a side room and stood behind the desk. He wore a dress shirt and tie, had a neatly trimmed beard, and his nametag said "Oliver."

"We're checking in," said Derek before Mrs. Murphy could answer.

She glanced at him with raised eyebrows. "I'll take care of it, Derek, unless you'd like to cover the bill."

Derek hastily stepped backward and waved his hand. "Please, after you. I insist."

Mrs. Murphy stepped up and smiled warmly at Oliver. "Hello. We have a reservation for two rooms. It's under the name Murphy." She passed over her driver's license and credit card. "We'd asked for them to be adjoining, if possible."

Oliver tapped at a keyboard and scanned his computer screen. "Murphy…" he said slowly, like he was searching for the name in a complex government database. Eventually, he nodded and looked up. "Yes, here we go. Two rooms…" He hesitated and glanced over at Sam and Derek, and then up at Mrs. Murphy. "I know you'd asked for rooms next to each other, but we'd had some of you in Room 403, and well…" Oliver cleared his throat and lowered his voice. "We probably don't want to put children in there."

Sam's ears perked up at the unusual answer. "What's wrong with 403?"

The man made a poor attempt to act casual. "Oh, well, it's nothing really…" He pecked again at his keyboard. "Some locals like to tell stories, that's all."

"What kind of stories?" asked Caitlin.

"It's not haunted, is it?" Derek practically yelled across the room.

Oliver hesitated a bit too long. "Well…"

Sam looked at Caitlin. What kind of town was this place? First, the catastrophe at the theater, and now a haunted room at the inn?

Mrs. Murphy laughed. "Oh, come on now, kids. There's no such thing as a haunted hotel room." She turned back to Oliver behind the desk. "How about a different floor? I'm sure you must have something with two rooms near each other."

His face relaxed as he nodded at the screen. "Yes, here we go. 321 and 318. They're just across the hall from each other on the third floor."

"That sounds great," said Mrs. Murphy. "Thank you."

Sam felt better about staying there, knowing that his room was ghost-free. Not that there were really such things as ghosts, but why even risk it? He wandered to the far wall and peeked into the next room. It was a library with luxurious leather couches, sitting chairs, and tall dark-colored wooden bookcases which ran from the floor all the way to the ceiling. A wooden ladder leaned up against the shelves to give access to the books near the top.

An old man sat at a square table by the window, intently studying the chessboard before him, like he was contemplating his next move. Sam tried not to be rude and stare, but it was odd to see someone playing chess by themselves. Maybe he'd been playing with Oliver before they'd arrived.

Just as Sam was about to turn around, the man glanced up. "Do you play?"

The question startled him. "Huh?"

"The game of chess. Do you play?"

"Um, a little, I guess, but not really."

The man huffed and stared back at the board. "What kind of answer is that? Either you do or you don't."

Sam knew how to play. His dad had taught Derek and him a couple of years ago. It had been kind of fun, but he wasn't very good yet. Certainly not good enough to want to play with some stranger in this potentially haunted inn. "We're just checking in."

"Were you all at the Barter tonight?" asked the man.

"We were." Sam glanced over his shoulder at the front desk. Mr. Murphy had joined the others in the lobby.

"Quite the commotion, I understand. Particularly with a world-famous performer in town."

"Huh? Oh, you mean Jake." Sam tried to think of how to describe all that had happened across the street at the theater. He decided to keep it simple. "They had to take him to the hospital."

The man groaned. "What a shame. Will he be okay?"

"I don't know. I mean, I hope so. He got hit pretty hard." Sam's mind started replaying the scene from the theater until someone called his name. He looked over his shoulder. Caitlin was waving to him as they picked up their bags and headed for the rooms. Sam turned to the man at the chessboard. "I've gotta go."

"Of course. Maybe later on then." The man gestured again to the game board.

Sam didn't know what to say to that. "Sure. Maybe."

CHAPTER SIX

The room was nice, except that Sam and Derek had to share a bed. It felt strange to be there without their mom and dad, but they'd spent so much time and even some vacations together with Caitlin's family. So it was almost as if they had substitute parents for the trip.

Caitlin was sleeping on a pull-out sofa in her parents' room across the hall, but unfortunately, the boys' room didn't have one of those. Derek had said Sam could sleep on the floor, but that seemed like a last resort. The bed in their room was queen-sized, but that only helped so much. Derek always accused Sam of snoring, and Derek tossed and turned and stole the covers. They were only staying for two nights, but Sam didn't hold high hopes for a great sleep.

"Where're the extra pillows?" Derek asked.

Sam pointed to the two already on the bed. "I think those are all we get."

His brother shook his head. "That won't work. I need at least three pillows. It helps keep my lumbar aligned."

"What are you even talking about?" He seriously didn't know where Derek came up with half the things that came out of his mouth.

"Don't you watch online infomercials, Sam?"

"No."

"Well, it's a proven fact. I'm going to go ask the guy at the front desk for some more. Come on, we'll bring Caitlin with us and look around. Maybe we'll even find that ghost."

As his brother stepped into the hall, Sam grabbed the room key. "Don't forget this."

"Good call, Sam. I knew you were here for a reason."

They picked up Caitlin from her room across the hall and then walked together down the main staircase.

"Isn't this just the coolest place?" Caitlin asked, as Derek stopped to ask Oliver for pillows. She walked over to the library doorway. "What were you looking at before in here?" Before Sam could answer, she gasped. "Wow, look at all these old books!"

Caitlin walked along the perimeter of the room, staring at the shelves filled with leather spines. She didn't notice the man sitting at the chessboard until she nearly bumped into him. "Oh, I'm sorry. I get a little carried away in places like this."

The man smiled and waved Sam over to the table. "I see you returned for our match."

Caitlin raised her eyebrows. "Oh, you've already met?"

Sam walked slowly over from the doorway. "Um, not really."

"I didn't know you played chess." Caitlin perched against the arm of a sofa and studied the board.

"Yeah, about that—" Sam replied, but the man was already resetting the board, moving the white and black pieces into opposing rows. He motioned to the chair at the other side of the table. "Please. Sit."

Caitlin nodded to Sam like he should do what the man said, so he reluctantly slid into the seat. "I'm not very good."

Before they could get started, Derek bounded over to them. "Oh, cool. Chess! I always kick Sam's butt."

Sam looked up and frowned. "You do not."

Derek laughed and waved to the old man. "Hi, I'm Derek."

The man nodded his head. "Alexi Bulgari. It's a pleasure." He glanced across the table like he was waiting for something.

Sam realized he'd forgotten to introduce himself. "Oh, right… Hi… I'm Sam. And this is Caitlin. Like I said before, we just checked in."

"From the play." Alexi seemed to be warming to them. "Welcome to The Martha."

"Thanks," said Derek, plopping onto the leather couch next to Caitlin. "Hey, you're not staying in Room 403, are you?"

The old man raised his bushy eyebrows. "You've heard about Beth, have you?"

"Beth?" asked Caitlin.

Sam had a sinking feeling in his stomach. "Who's that?"

Alexi leaned back in his chair, shifting his focus from the chessboard. He flashed them a creepy smile. "Surely, you've heard the stories?"

Derek shook his head and inched closer. "No, we just got here. But the front desk dude said we shouldn't stay in Room 403."

"Oliver said it was because of local stories," added Caitlin. "Do you know what he's talking about?"

"I suppose the match can wait." Alexi turned his chair closer to the couch. He seemed to be enjoying educating the new young guests. "I'm sure you'd rather hear a love story than play chess."

"A love story?" Derek made a face and sank back into the sofa. "I thought it was going to be a ghost story."

Alexi chuckled. "Fear not. It's a tragic love story. I don't think you'll be disappointed. It's often known as the tale of the Yankee Sweetheart."

Derek grunted. "Okay, I guess. I do like the Yankees. Maybe it'll be about Babe Ruth."

Caitlin smacked Derek's knee. "Quiet. I want to hear the story." She nodded back at Alexi. "Please, tell us."

Alexi grinned and spread his arms wide. "This place was once a girls' school named Martha Washington College. But during the Civil War, it served as a hospital for injured soldiers from both armies. Some students stayed on as nurses. One such girl was named Beth, and she came to care for a young officer named Captain John Stoves."

"I don't think I have ever heard of him. I thought you said he was on the Yankees?" interrupted Derek.

"Yankee means he was a soldier from the northern Union Army," said Caitlin. "Now, let's listen."

Alexi nodded. "Captain Stoves was badly wounded and captured by the Confederate Army. They placed him in Room 403, where Nurse Beth cared for him over several weeks. During that time, the two fell deeply in love, and Beth would often play her violin for Captain Stoves to ease his pain."

"That's so sweet," Caitlin whispered.

Sam glanced at her on the couch. She seemed to really be getting into this story. "So what happened? Did they get married?"

Alexi shook his head solemnly. "Alas, it was not meant to be. His injuries were too severe."

Derek looked up. "The captain died?"

Alexi nodded. "But in his final moments, he called out for Beth, asking her to play him one last song."

Oh brother, thought Sam.

"But before she could get her violin and play, he slipped away."

Caitlin gasped. "Oh, no."

"There was nothing for Beth to do but play one last,

sweet Southern melody. When a guard entered the room to see if the captain was able to be taken to the military court, the heartbroken young nurse exclaimed that her love had been pardoned by an officer higher than General Lee. Captain Stoves was dead."

"That's quite a story," said Caitlin.

"Wasn't there supposed to be a ghost in this story?" asked Derek impatiently.

"What happened to Beth?" asked Sam.

Alexi stared out the window. "Poor Beth died of typhoid fever shortly after. But many think that she never really left Room 403."

Sam didn't like where this story was going. "What do you mean?"

"For years after the war, students at the college, and later, guests and staff at the inn, have heard Beth's violin playing softly in the night. Many believe that she still visits Room 403 to comfort her lost Yankee soldier."

Sam turned to his brother. "Still want to stay in Room 403?"

Derek hesitated, but then stood confidently. "Sure, I mean, it's only a little violin music. What's the worst that could happen?"

Alexi chuckled. "This town is full of stories. I am sure we could find one that is more to your liking, young man. Have you never visited Abingdon before your play at the Barter?"

Caitlin explained how they'd driven from Richmond

to see her aunt Ginny and Jacob Greensboro, only to have the play cut short.

"Sounds like Mr. Porterfield is having some fun today as well," Alexi replied.

Sam shook his head. "Don't tell me the Barter's haunted, too."

Alexi shrugged. "Like I told you, a town as old as this one has a story for just about every place along Main Street."

"What do they say about the Barter?" asked Derek.

Alexi looked out the window. "Some say they've seen Porterfield show up to watch performances over the years since his death."

"How do they know it's him?" asked Caitlin.

"He always sits in his favorite seat in the left opera box up in the balcony," Alexi explained. "And of course, he's wearing his signature white three-piece suit."

Sam's elbow slipped off the table and knocked several chess pieces to the floor.

"What's the matter, kid?" Alexi asked. "You look like you've seen a ghost."

Sam leaned back and tried to breathe.

"Sam?" Caitlin reached down and picked up the fallen chess pieces. "What's wrong?"

He glanced over at the others. "I saw him, remember? The man in the white three-piece suit in the balcony. He was walking down the aisle just before the set crashed down on the stage. That's what I was trying to tell you guys before."

"Wait a minute," said Derek. "You're telling me you saw Robert Porterfield's ghost in the theater?" He cackled. "That's pretty out there, Sam. Even for you."

Sam tried to collect his thoughts. Between the story about Beth and the Yankee soldier and now this news about Robert Porterfield's ghost, it was hard to distinguish what was really true. "I don't know exactly what I saw, but there was someone there and he was wearing white."

Alexi stroked his beard slowly. "Theaters are known for their spectral guests. That's what the ghost lights are for."

"What kind of light?" asked Derek.

"A ghost light. Every theater has one."

"That can't be real," said Sam.

Alexi shrugged. "I agree that some things are hard to know for certain, but I assure you that a ghost light is real."

"What is it for?" asked Caitlin.

"Mostly, a simple practical reason," Alexi answered. "The last person to leave the theater has to turn out the lights, but the ghost light always stays on just to keep anyone from fumbling around in the dark and hurting themselves."

Sam frowned. "So, it's just for safety, then." That didn't sound so scary. Maybe they should just call it the safety light.

"Unless there are some things that never leave," Derek

whispered in a creepy voice. He looked at Alexi with expectation. "Am I right?"

Alexi chuckled. "Perhaps."

Caitlin's phone buzzed and she clicked on a video call. "Hi, Mom."

"There you are." Mrs. Murphy's voice came from the speaker. "I was wondering where you three had run off to. Everything okay?"

"Yeah, Mom." Caitlin panned her phone across the room. "We're just down in the library talking with Mr. Bulagwi—"

"Bulgari," he corrected.

Caitlin grimaced. "Oh, sorry. Mr. Bulgari. He was just telling us stories about the town's past. You know how much we love history."

Mrs. Murphy laughed. "I do know that. But I also know it's getting late. Remember, we're still planning to bike the Creeper Trail tomorrow morning. How about you all head back up to the rooms?"

"Okay. We'll be up in a minute." Caitlin ended the call and shrugged to Alexi. "Looks like we have to leave. Thanks for the stories."

"Enjoy the hotel." Alexi bowed his head and motioned to Sam. "Perhaps we can play our game tomorrow."

Sam didn't know about that, but he tried to be polite. "Sure. Goodnight."

Derek nudged him. "Aren't you going to say goodnight?"

Sam gave him a blank look. "I just did."

"No, not to him." Derek flashed a mischievous grin. "To Beth. I think she has a thing for you."

Alexi broke out into a hearty laugh as Sam stood and brushed past Derek toward the lobby. "Give me a break."

CHAPTER SEVEN

S am, Derek, and Caitlin started the trek up the winding main staircase beside the lobby. The wooden boards under the carpet creaked loudly under each footstep. Sam patted his pockets, trying to find where he'd put their room keycard. He nearly ran into Derek, who had stopped on the top landing. "Watch out, will you?"

"I think we went too far, guys," called Caitlin from behind them. "Our rooms are on the third floor, remember?"

Derek turned around slowly, his eyes wide. He pointed to the doorway ahead of them and whispered. "But look where we are."

They followed his glance to the number on the door. Room 403. The door was cracked open just an inch, and the room inside was dark.

Sam shook his head. "Very funny. Stop trying to scare

us. It was just a story." The truth was, he didn't know what to think about the creepy story of the Yankee Sweethearts or the reports of people hearing violin music. But he definitely knew he wanted nothing to do with that room.

Caitlin glanced over at him. "Aren't you curious?"

"No, not really. I prefer rooms that aren't haunted."

Derek held up his hand. "Do you hear that?"

Sam pushed his brother away. "Stop."

"Stop what? I'm not kidding." Derek leaned closer to the open door. "Listen."

Sam didn't want to admit to it, but he did hear something. Faint music played from somewhere inside the dark room. He turned and pointed to his brother's pocket. He wasn't going to fall for another one of his tricks. "I know it's just your phone."

Derek held his phone up in his hands to prove that it was silent.

Caitlin stood frozen. "I hear it too. Is it coming from inside the room?"

Sam glanced down the hall. "Okay, this has been fun, but you heard your mom. It's time for bed." Scary stories were kind of funny, but this was where he drew the line.

He was about to walk back down the stairs when a low groan sounded from Room 403. They watched in horror as the door drifted open another inch. Or at least it seemed like it did. It was hard to tell.

"Tell me you saw that," whispered Derek.

"Maybe the A/C just came on," said Sam. "This is an

old building. It probably makes lots of noises. Things like that happen all the time." Maybe all of their imaginations were working overtime.

Caitlin took a tentative step forward. "Come on, I want to see what's going on in there."

"Why exactly?" asked Sam.

"Think about the story." Caitlin leaned toward the darkness. "How do you think Beth must have felt, watching the man she loved die? And this is the room where it took place."

"I don't know," said Derek. "Caitlin, how would you feel if Sam died?"

Sam slugged his brother in the shoulder, but Caitlin ignored them and pushed at the door. "I just want to take a look. Hello?"

Sam took a deep breath and reluctantly followed her into the darkness. "This is stupid."

"I'm right behind you," whispered Derek.

From the faint light from the hall, they could see a bed in the middle of the room. The music seemed to come from near the window. Sam stepped cautiously toward the foot of the bed. He heard Derek's footsteps behind him, and he turned around just in time to see his older brother's mischievous grin from the hallway.

Then the door slammed shut.

Sam jumped so high he thought his head might touch the ceiling. "Derek! Open the door!"

Obnoxious laugher spilled through the door from the hall. "Do you see Beth?"

Sam lunged for the door, but bumped into Caitlin in the darkness. "Ow. Sorry. I can't see anything."

"Derek, open the door right now," Caitlin called. "It's not funny."

"Oh, come on. Take a joke, will you?" Derek answered. They heard the door handle jingle, but it didn't open. "Did you lock it?"

Sam tried to stay calm. He didn't want to freak out in front of Caitlin. She probably felt the same as him and it wouldn't help to have both of them panicking. But they were locked in the dark in haunted Room 403! Was it his imagination, or was the violin music getting louder?

"No, we didn't lock it," answered Caitlin. "We're just standing here in the dark."

Derek rattled the handle again, but the door still didn't open. "Well, it's not turning. Maybe I need a key."

Sam felt his blood pressure rising. "Maybe you need a brain. Open the door, Derek! Right now!"

"Do you see a keycard in there?"

"It's pitch black," Caitlin cried. "We can't see anything."

"Well, try the door from your side. Maybe it will open."

Caitlin reached over and took Sam's hand. "Just so we don't get lost," she assured him.

"Right." They inched forward, their free arms outstretched until they touched the wall. Sam let go of Caitlin's hand and felt along the wall until he found the door handle. It still wouldn't turn. "Are you sure you're not holding it?"

"I guess I'll have to go find Oliver," said Derek. "Do you think you two can behave in there until I get back?"

"Shut up!" Sam yelled. "Just hurry." He was going to kill his brother whenever they got out.

Caitlin let out a nervous chuckle. "It's not really haunted, you know. That's just a silly story."

Sam peered across the room in the darkness. "Of course I know that. But where's the music coming from? There has to be a light switch somewhere."

Caitlin's hands patted at the wall until suddenly the room filled with light. "Got it!"

Sam blinked at the brightness. "Thanks." He noticed a small alarm clock radio on the nightstand by the window. He groaned and when he tapped the power button, the music stopped. "That's a mean joke. Now let's get out of here."

He turned to head for the door, but Caitlin held up her hand. "Wait. Listen. Do you hear that?"

Sam shook his head. "It wasn't funny the first time."

"No, not music. It sounds like someone's talking. Listen." Caitlin stepped to the wall and leaned toward an air vent. "I think it's coming from down here." She knelt with her ear to the vent. "I think someone's talking about the play."

"What are they saying?"

Caitlin put her finger to her lips and waved Sam down to the floor. He crouched next to her and strained to hear the words echoing through the metal. It sounded like a man talking on the phone, because he could only hear one side of a conversation.

"I don't know his status yet, but they took him out on a stretcher."

They were talking about Jake! Sam looked up and considered the vent. There was no telling where the duct system could lead to in the old hotel. The voice might be in the next room, or it could be on a different floor. Caitlin waved him back down.

"Yeah, it wasn't exactly to plan, but it could still work out to our advantage," the voice continued. "Greensboro being out of the picture actually makes it more expedient. I'll meet you at—"

Loud voices came from the hallway and a keycard beeped. The room's door burst open. Sam and Caitlin banged heads as they turned quickly to see Derek standing with Oliver.

Derek stared down at them with amusement. "And what might you two be doing?"

They quickly jumped up from the floor. Sam felt his face growing red.

"You kids aren't supposed to be in here," growled Oliver.

Derek held up his hand. "I told them and told them, but you know how it is—young love just won't be denied."

"Oh my gosh," said Sam.

Caitlin smiled apologetically as her face turned the

same color as Sam's. "We're sorry, the door locked by accident."

"Yeah," added Sam. "We heard music playing inside the room, and we wanted to see what was going on. Then my brother here shoved us in and locked the door."

Oliver's lips tightened and he put his hand to his forehead. "Rosa. What am I going to do with her?"

Caitlin lowered her eyebrows. "Rosa? I thought the Yankee Sweetheart's name was Beth."

"Rosa is the housekeeper who cleans this floor," Oliver explained. "She thinks it's funny to leave music playing on the radio, despite what I tell her."

"Oh," muttered Sam. That made more sense than an actual haunted room. He glanced back at the vent. "Do you know who's in the next room?"

Oliver shook his head. "I'm afraid I can't share that type of information." He pointed at the hallway. "Isn't it past your bedtime?"

They apologized again and walked down the staircase to the third floor. Lingering in the doorway of Caitlin's room, Sam told Derek what they'd heard in the vent.

"Who do you think it was?" Derek asked.

Caitlin glanced inside the room at her parents and then back to the boys in the hall. "I don't know, but we need to find out."

CHAPTER EIGHT

W aking up the next morning proved Sam had been right to dread sharing a bed with Derek. It felt like he'd barely slept a wink with all his brother's tossing and turning. His brain was still half asleep, but he vaguely sensed morning light coming in from the window.

The sound of peaceful music played faintly nearby. After the long drive the day before with Caitlin and her guitar playing, he was used to music in the background. He nearly drifted back to sleep, but something tugged at his mind. That wasn't guitar music he heard. It was more like… a violin!

Sam bolted upright in his bed. He rubbed his eyes until he could focus on someone by the window. Derek was cracking up at the music playing from his phone. "What's the matter, Sam? Beth didn't scare you, did she?"

Sam reached for one of the extra pillows strewn across

the bed and tossed it toward the window. Derek ducked and it bounced against the glass. "Leave me alone, will you?"

"Didn't you sleep well?"

"No, and I wonder why." Sam had one foot on the floor when a knock sounded at the door. "What now?"

"Maybe it's room service."

Sam slid back onto the bed as Derek walked to the door. "Did you order something?"

"Well, no, but maybe it's included." Derek opened the door to a familiar voice.

"Good morning," Caitlin said from the hall.

Sam pulled the covers up over his shoulders and wondered if his hair was standing on end. That often happened when he first woke up.

"Oh, hi," Derek answered. "I'd invite you in, but Sam's naked." His voice lowered to a whisper. "Don't ask me why, but he often likes to sleep in the nude."

"Oh…" Caitlin said quickly.

"What?" Sam yelled out. "I do not."

"Sorry, I can come back."

"I'm not naked, Caitlin. I'm just still in bed."

Derek chuckled. "Trust me, it's almost as bad. You don't want to catch Sam first thing in the morning. It's not a pretty sight."

"Shut up, will you?" Sam pulled the covers a little higher and ran his fingers through his hair. "What's up? You can come in."

Caitlin peeked cautiously around the corner like she wasn't convinced.

Sam sighed. "I told you, I'm not naked."

When she saw him beneath the covers, she stepped a little closer and giggled. "I just wanted to see if you're ready to go get breakfast. My dad says we're leaving soon for the Creeper Trail."

"I'm ready, but...," Derek glanced back at the bed, "he might be a while."

Sam shook his head. "You guys go ahead. I'll be down in five minutes." He was excited about going biking. He could shower when they got back.

As Derek followed Caitlin into the hall, he stopped and called back into the room. "Remember, Sam, they require clothing at breakfast."

Sam grabbed another pillow and hurled it at the closing door.

BREAKFAST WAS SERVED in the restaurant located one floor below the ground floor lobby. Somewhere in the hotel there was a pool, spa, tennis courts, and lots of other things, but Sam didn't know if they'd have time to check any of those out on this trip. The dining room was buzzing with activity and conversation. Perhaps many of the guests had also been at the Barter the night before. Sam spotted Derek and Caitlin carrying plates of food from a buffet. They sat at a round table in the middle of the room with Caitlin's parents.

"Morning, Sam." Mrs. Murphy pushed in her chair like she was leaving. "Help yourself. We're just going back up to the room to finish getting ready."

Derek pointed to the buffet line. "They have waffles!"

Sam's stomach rumbled loudly, and Mrs. Murphy laughed. "We'll let you get to it, then. Sounds like you're hungry."

"The bike outfitter shuttle should be collecting us outside in the driveway in about fifteen minutes," Mr. Murphy reminded them. "We'll meet you on the porch."

When Sam came back to the table, his plate was filled with a pile of tasty goodness slathered in syrup. Caitlin's aunt was now seated next to Caitlin and Derek.

"Hungry much?" Derek chuckled, looking at Sam's loaded plate.

"Yeah," he replied and swiftly shoveled a fork full of waffles into his mouth.

"Good morning, Sam," said Ginny. "Your brother tells me you saw an apparition last night."

Sam shot Derek a glare as he finished chewing. "No, it was just somebody's idea of a joke to play violin music on the radio. And someone else decided to lock us in. Apparently, everybody's a comedian around here." He wiped his mouth with a napkin. It was one thing for his brother to be his usual obnoxious self, but did he have to tell everyone else about it, too?

Derek snickered but shook his head. "I didn't tell her about Beth."

"I was referring to last night at the Barter," Ginny clarified. "Your brother said that you saw something on the balcony before the show stopped? I also remembered you were telling me about seeing a sandbag fall before I had to go last night."

"Oh..." Sam had almost forgotten about that with everything else going on. "Well, yeah. I mean, I think so." He explained again how he'd seen the man in the white three-piece suit just before the sandbag crashed into the back of the stage. "I tried to yell, but it was too late."

"Now that you mention it, I thought I'd heard something just before the accident." Ginny seemed to take Sam's words seriously. "The detective who arrived with Bernard is investigating the incident. He's looking at the set pieces and the sandbag ropes. It's possible he'll want to speak with you. It's hard for me to imagine that someone would intentionally do something like that, but we did have that threatening letter delivered to Jake's dressing room. There are all kinds of people out there."

"That's for sure," Sam muttered, glancing at his brother as he gulped down another big bite. He didn't want to have to talk to the police about what had happened. He could barely keep things straight in his own mind.

"Do you think it was Porterfield's ghost?" asked Derek. "A guy in the library here told us all about him last night."

"You don't believe in that kind of stuff, do you, Aunt Ginny?" asked Caitlin.

Ginny leaned away from the table and cocked her head. "I'm not one to believe in ghost stories. Tales about this town have been passed around for as long as I can remember, and I've always dismissed them as folks with overactive imaginations. But lately…" She looked like she was trying to think of what to say next.

"Lately what?" asked Derek.

"Did you see something too?" Sam asked mid-bite. If someone like Ginny had seen the ghost, maybe he wasn't crazy after all.

"It's hard to tell what is real, what is shadows, or what's just your mind playing tricks. But I've seen and heard things late at night while getting ready for this production that are hard to explain. The Barter has a lot of connections to this old inn, and nearly as many stories to go with it."

"Does Beth play violin music over there too?" asked Derek.

Ginny laughed nervously. "No, but there is a tunnel that connects the inn with the theater."

Derek raised his head. "A tunnel? It's just like the Jefferson! There aren't any alligators, are there?"

Sam felt his heart skip a beat at the mention of the historic hotel in downtown Richmond. They'd stayed there once before for a wedding. It had a long history of alligators living in the lobby fountains, and they'd found more than they'd bargained for in a passage that ran under the hotel.

"Alligators?" Ginny looked surprised. "Goodness, I hope not! Why would you ask that?"

Sam gulped as Derek waved his hand. "No reason."

Ginny narrowed her eyes. "The theater building was originally constructed in the 1830s as a Presbyterian church. The Confederate Army built a tunnel during the war to shuttle ammunition, soldiers, and the wounded."

"Is it still there?" asked Caitlin.

Ginny nodded. "A door in the corner of our wardrobe room leads right to it. But no one's used it since a cave-in shortly after the war. Over the years, any attempts to make repairs have sent more than a few contractors running in fear and swearing they wouldn't come back. Some of them didn't even stop to grab their tools."

"What were they afraid of?" asked Caitlin. "Did they just not like tunnels?"

Ginny glanced around the room and then back at the kids. "Legend says that the Union Army killed two Confederate soldiers in the tunnel who were caught smuggling weapons. Ever since, their spirits have cast a frightening presence in that place."

Derek leaned closer as he took in her words. "Have you gone in there?"

Ginny's face turned serious. "I have not, and I have no plans to, either."

That was enough for Sam. If Ginny didn't have a

reason to go into that tunnel, then they certainly did not either.

Derek didn't seem so convinced. "We might have to look into that if we're going to solve the case."

"Derek—" Sam started, but his brother held his hand up.

"You don't think it's a coincidence that we were here when all this happened, do you? We're supposed to help solve this mystery."

Ginny smiled. "That's nice of you to offer, Derek, but I'm sure the police will soon have things well in hand. You three don't need to worry about it. I'm just sorry your visit hasn't worked out as planned."

"It's okay, Aunt Ginny," said Caitlin. "We know it's been even harder on you."

"Do you know how Jake's doing?" asked Sam, trying to change the subject.

Ginny bit her lip. "I'll head over to the hospital today to check on his condition. I've been fielding texts from his agent and the press for hours."

"What about the other guy who walked in with the policeman last night when we left?" asked Derek. "The rich dude who looked like he was about to burst a blood vessel."

"Bernard Hostetter?" Ginny took a sip of her coffee. "Oh, Bernard always makes things interesting. He runs WHI—Wolf Hills Investments. They're mostly focused on real estate, but the theater has been in dire straits the past few years. We had to look for financing anywhere we could get it. With no other options, last month we sold WHI a forty-nine percent stake in the theater. Even with the deal, we only had just enough capital to keep us going through the rest of the year. Bernard was pressing for more, but the board refused to give him a controlling interest."

Sam tried to follow what Ginny was saying about how the finances of a theater worked, but it sounded complicated.

"Operating the Barter is a daily adventure. It has expenses like any old building, everything from the heat, outdated electrical wiring, and lots of maintenance to keep everything in tip-top shape. Even in a normal season, keeping things humming isn't easy. But it's been even more of a struggle to get back to a full production schedule after the shutdowns in recent years."

"But doesn't the state own the theater?" asked Caitlin. "The sign out front calls it 'The State Theatre of Virginia.'"

Ginny chuckled. "That's mostly in name only. We rely on donations from patrons and other benefactors to keep the building running. Our productions are almost entirely self-funded. Getting any production up and running requires a lot of investment and capital. This one especially so with a big name like Jacob Greensboro on the marquee."

"He's not performing for free?" asked Sam. "I mean, since this is where he got his start and all?"

Ginny nearly choked on her coffee. "No. He is not.

Let's just say that Mr. Greensboro was well compensated for those sixty minutes on the stage last night. And while Bernard's funding has helped make it all possible, he's a demanding investor. Sometimes I think he's more interested in seeing healthy profits than he is in sustaining the arts. But this is nothing new. The arts have struggled since back in William Shakespeare's day to balance their costs."

Caitlin frowned. "But the arts are important."

Ginny patted her arm. "You don't have to remind me about that, dear."

"She wants to be a country music singer," Derek blurted out.

Caitlin's eyes widened, and she turned and stared at Derek. "I'm learning to play the guitar."

"Is that right?" Ginny replied. "That's wonderful."

"And she's writing songs."

Caitlin's cheeks reddened. "Derek…"

Ginny smiled. "It's okay, honey. It takes a lot of courage to be creative, let alone perform in front of others."

"She's pretty good," added Sam, trying to say something supportive. "Maybe she can play at the Barter."

Caitlin laughed nervously. "I don't think I'm ready for that yet."

"Well, I have no doubt that you'll be successful." Ginny stood and pushed in her chair. She reached out and hugged Caitlin. "You've grown into quite the accomplished young lady."

"Thanks."

A song started playing on Ginny's phone. Sam didn't recognize it, but the singer was shouting about a house burning down. Ginny answered. "Okay, they'll be right out."

She set the phone back on the table. "That was your father. He said they're ready outside. Did I hear you're all going biking?"

"Oh, yeah. We're supposed to meet the shuttle," said Caitlin.

Sam pointed to the phone. "What was that ring tone?"

Ginny laughed. "Oh, that's an old Talking Heads song that we used to play at the end of rehearsals." As Caitlin and Derek stood and turned to leave, she called out to them quickly. "And, kids, one more thing."

Caitlin turned back to her aunt. "Yeah?"

"Don't worry about the theater. It'll all work itself out."

Caitlin nodded solemnly. "Okay. I sure hope so."

Derek pointed to the door. "Come on, Sam. Or are you going back for seconds?"

Sam washed his last bite of waffles down with a swig of orange juice. "Ready."

CHAPTER NINE

A white passenger van was parked on the circle driveway that ran along The Martha's front porch. Bright images of bike wheels and the name *Creeper Bikes* decorated the side panels. Oversized metal racks were mounted on the roof, off the back bumper, and even out in the front.

"So, what's the deal with the name?" asked Sam as they lined up to get seats.

"Creeper Bikes?" said Caitlin. "Probably because of the trail, Sam."

Derek chuckled. "And you think *I* don't pay attention…"

Sam rolled his eyes. "No, not the shuttle. I mean the trail. Why is it called the Creeper Trail?"

"Beats me." Derek climbed into the open van door and slid into the back row. "It sounds like the hunting grounds of some kind of serial killer. Like the Boston

Strangler or something. Maybe he picks people up in this van and takes them deep into the woods to—"

Mr. Murphy cleared his voice loudly. "I think we get the idea."

"Virginia Creeper." Caitlin turned to her parents. "It's the name of a plant, isn't it? Maybe there are lots of those plants on the trail."

"I'm actually not sure," Mrs. Murphy answered. "But you could be right. I think it's a vine, maybe?"

Sam glanced back at the hotel and shivered. "This whole town is giving me the creeps."

The shuttle driver slid the door closed and walked around to his seat. He introduced himself as Franklin, and before starting the engine, he swiveled around to face them. "Couldn't help but overhear your conversation. That's one of the most common questions I get from folks—the origin of the trail name."

"Which of us was right?" asked Caitlin.

"Was it a killer," said Derek, "or just a plant?"

Franklin chuckled. "Well, as far as I know, it wasn't a killer."

"Ha!" Sam elbowed Derek in the ribs. "You're wrong."

Derek frowned. "He said 'as far as he knows.' I could still be right."

Mrs. Murphy waved for them to be quiet. "So it was a plant, then?"

"In a way," Franklin explained. "There *is* a common vine in these parts called Virginia Creeper. But the trail name has more to do with trains than plants. It's built on an old railroad bed from the late 1800s. The trains that wound their way up the steep, twisting mountain route were called Virginia Creepers. Now *that* name may have originated from the plant, but it was a fitting title for those hard-working trains that pushed over those ranges filled with passengers and supplies."

Derek scratched his head as the driver faced forward and started the engine. "Huh. I'd never have guessed it was trains."

"Trains changed the game in this country for expansion into the West, and Abingdon was plumb in the middle of it. Even before the trains, this area that leads toward the Cumberland Gap was called The Great Road. It became one of the main crossing points over the Appalachians for early pioneers heading west."

"Wow," said Mrs. Murphy. "I never knew that. And I grew up in Virginia!"

"Are there still trains running?" asked Caitlin.

"Not on the trail route," answered Franklin. "They don't mix well with the bikers, you know." He stopped to chuckle at his joke. "Last one ran back in 1977. After that, they pulled up the tracks and the Forest Service started buying up the land to convert it to a rails-to-trails initiative."

"That's just like High Bridge Trail I drove you three to up near Farmville," said Mr. Murphy.

"Oh yeah, that was fun," said Caitlin.

Derek smirked at Sam. "This time, try to keep your

glasses on your face."

Sam frowned and self-consciously pushed the plastic frame higher on his nose as he turned toward the window. "This time we're staying on the trail."

"What's our route today?" Mrs. Murphy asked.

"We'll stop off at our shop in Damascus and get y'all fitted with bikes and helmets. Then we'll head all the way out to Whitetop, the Creeper's eastern trailhead."

"Is it far?" Sam remembered being pretty tired after pedaling the long, flat High Bridge Trail.

Franklin leaned forward to check the traffic both ways before turning left. "The Creeper's thirty-four miles, but you'll just be doing seventeen of it today."

"That still seems a ways…" said Mrs. Murphy.

"Nah, you'll be fine," said Franklin. "Whitetop to Damascus is a nice, steady downgrade. Not a lot of pedaling. It's a perfect time to enjoy the scenery. The trail takes you through just about everything—farmland and open fields, river crossing trestles, wooded areas—it's beautiful. And I'm not just saying that because they pay me to. Riding the trail is one of my favorite things to do on my days off."

"Maybe if Little Red Riding Hood had a bike, she'd have been able to beat the wolf to Grandma's house," said Sam, thinking back to the play.

"Yeah, but he'd still huff and puff and blow the house down," said Derek. "Or at least topple the set pieces."

Caitlin laughed. "That was a different story."

"It wasn't Little Red Riding Hood?" asked Derek.

"No, it was the Three Little Pigs."

"Oh, yeah," said Derek.

"Why are there so many stories about wolves?" Sam watched out the van window as they left the town of Abingdon behind.

* * *

AFTER THEY STOPPED at the outfitter shop in Damascus, they piled back into the van with several other groups and everyone's bikes loaded on. Franklin talked nearly the whole way up the mountain. "I have a hard time sitting in silence," he called from the front. "So I figure it's a good time to give instructions and a bit of the area's history. Hope you don't mind."

Sam was squeezed between Caitlin and Derek in the back row of the van, and he had a hard time paying attention to Franklin's history lessons because he quickly became carsick. The road up to Whitetop wound back and forth up the mountain for nearly thirty minutes.

"I read that the Forest Service did a lot of work in this area," said Mr. Murphy from the middle row.

"Sure did," answered Franklin. "But it started with the railroads. Just like out west, the big timber companies flowed into this area, clearing the mountainsides of virgin forests. At one point in the early 1900s, this area of Virginia around Washington County was harvesting more lumber—oak, pine, poplar, and chestnut—than all of Pennsylvania."

"They cut down all the trees?" Caitlin gasped. "That's terrible."

"There was a twenty-five-year lumber boom until the US Forest Service grew in power and acquired most of the land around Damascus for conservation and restoration."

"Thank goodness," said Caitlin.

Sam held his stomach and wondered if this was what it would have felt like being on one of the Creeper trains. But at least those went slowly. Franklin made this trip a dozen times a day and hit each of the curves at full speed. Sam's stomach did a somersault on every switchback. He finally just closed his eyes and tried to take deep breaths.

"You okay?" asked Caitlin.

"Uh-huh. Just tell me when we get there."

It seemed like they'd never reach the mountaintop, but eventually Sam heard the van pull into a gravel parking lot. He was the last one off the shuttle and immediately bent over to inhale the fresh mountain air.

"Lookin' a little green there, son." Franklin chuckled as he wheeled Sam's bike over to him. "You gonna be all right?"

Sam stood up and gripped the handlebars. "Yeah, just a little carsick. Thanks."

Caitlin's mom took her bike from Franklin and strapped on her helmet. "How long does the ride usually take?"

"Depends on how eager you are." He smirked at Derek. "But most folks like to take their time. My wife likes to stop at some of the little stands along the way and do some souvenir shopping or grab a snack and stretch her legs. If you do that, it's usually two or three hours."

Sam was starting to feel better now that he was out of the van, so the idea of snacks sounded pretty good. He swung his leg over the crossbar and tested the brakes on his bike. If the ride was all downhill, those would be pretty important.

Caitlin pulled up next to him. "You ready?"

Sam nodded. "Let's do it."

"Wanna race down the hill?" asked Derek.

"I think we'll stay together today," said Mr. Murphy, a small backpack strapped on his shoulders with an extra water bottle and a first-aid kit.

"Oh, I nearly forgot…" Derek steadied his feet on the ground and then dramatically stripped off his sweatshirt. He sported a sleeveless T-shirt with a picture of Bigfoot and the words *I BELIEVE* blazed across the front. "Now I'm ready."

Sam let a laugh escape, despite himself. "Where did you get that?"

"Back in the shop. I think we go… that way." He flexed his biceps and swiveled his hand around so that it pointed down the trail.

"Oh brother," Sam muttered as everyone else laughed. "I believe you've finally lost your mind."

"We can get you one when we get back," called Derek, rushing past them onto the trail. "Come on!"

CHAPTER TEN

Franklin had been right. The Creeper Trail wasn't a very hard ride. Without being steep, the steady downgrade made the dirt and gravel trail one of the easiest rides Sam had ever been on. Their group of five traveled in a single-file line, winding their way down the wooded trail. Mr. Murphy insisted that he lead to prevent Derek from speeding off ahead of everyone. Caitlin came next, followed by Mrs. Murphy, Sam, and then finally Derek in the rear. They rode ten to twenty feet apart from each other, although Derek insisted on pulling up on Sam's back tire several times just to act like he was going to knock him into the woods.

Most of the trail hugged a stream winding its way down the mountain. It was probably what the builders had used years ago to map out the original rail line. Whenever possible, Sam tried to watch the river. Sometimes it was level to the trail, and at other spots it sunk into a valley below. He glimpsed several sections with white water swirling over the rocks below small waterfalls. He couldn't stare for too long though, or else he'd veer off the trail.

Thick patches of rhododendron bushes and wide rock ledges alternated with thickets of evergreens to keep them cool and shaded most of the way. It was hard to believe that years ago the entire mountainside had been clear-cut of all the trees for timber sales. Dozens of small wooden bridges made a patchwork along the route as the trail crossed back and forth over the stream. On the far side of one bridge, a man stepped into the water in tall wader boots with a fly rod. He waved his line gently back and forth above the water like a magic wand until it settled silently along the top of the stream, a fly on a hook designed to tempt an unsuspecting trout.

Up ahead, Sam saw a clearing with a small building and a trailer with colorful signs. He remembered Franklin talking about places for snacks and he called ahead to Caitlin. "I think that's one of those places to eat." Even without hard pedaling, bike riding always worked up his appetite.

"How am I not surprised you remembered that?" Derek said, pulling next to him.

"Can we stop here?" Caitlin shouted ahead to her dad.

Sam smiled when Mr. Murphy signaled for a stop. Their bike line pulled into the clearing on the side of the trail and stopped by a small building with picnic tables outside.

"Ready for a break?" Caitlin's dad asked.

"Shocker," said Derek, "but Sam's starving."

Mrs. Murphy stretched down to touch her toes. "I think it's a great time to stop, Sam."

They rested their bikes along a slope and went inside to browse some local arts and crafts and little trinkets. Mr. Murphy treated them to snacks—Sam got a hot dog, the others bought chips, a pretzel, trail mix, and drinks. They walked outside to a picnic table and soaked in the sounds of the forest and the rushing stream in the distance.

As they ate, two guys emerged from the trees. They crossed the Creeper Trail and walked toward the small store. Both carried tall backpacks on their shoulders, and the taller of the two had his shirt off and looked strong.

Sam turned and couldn't help but notice Caitlin's eyes following them across the grass. "I wonder where they're going?" she asked.

Mrs. Murphy smiled. "I can invite them over to join us for lunch if you'd like, honey?"

Caitlin swatted at the air and blushed. "Mom, stop it."

Before she could say anything further, the younger of the two boys, who seemed to be about Derek's age, walked to the second picnic table. He dropped his heavy pack next to them on the ground with a thud and then collapsed flat on his back onto the table.

"You okay?" asked Mr. Murphy.

The boy turned his head and opened one eye. He looked surprised, like he hadn't noticed them. He pulled himself upright and hung his legs over the side of the table. "I'm sorry, didn't mean to disturb your lunch. Guess I'm more tired than I thought."

"You guys hiking?" asked Derek.

"The pack gave it away, didn't it?" The boy grinned and wiped his face with his T-shirt. "Sorry for the smell. We've been out on the trail for nearly a week."

"Are you following the Creeper Trail?" asked Sam.

"Nah, we're sticking to the AT, but they intersect for a bit here near Damascus."

"The AT?" said Derek.

"The Appalachian Trail," Caitlin blurted, unable to hold back from showing off her knowledge. "Remember? We hiked on it up by Swannanoa. It has the white blaze on the trees."

The boy smiled at Caitlin. "Very good."

Derek held up his finger. "That's where I fought off the bear."

The boy raised his eyebrows in surprise. "Really?"

Sam shook his head. "He didn't fight the bear. It ate our lunch on the trail. He just took its picture."

Derek shrugged. "It was a good picture."

Mr. Murphy nodded. "I remember that one all right." He looked over at the boy. "You guys thru-hiking?"

"Nah, just section hiking. The AT winds across the mountain and runs right through Main Street in Damascus. We're working our way back up to Shenandoah. Our dad's a ranger in the national park."

The other boy walked up behind them and nodded. Unlike Derek, he looked like he could actually fight off a bear if he had to. "My little brother's not talking your ear off, is he?"

"Probably just scaring them with my foul smells." The first boy made a face and laughed.

"Not at all," said Mrs. Murphy. "We were just asking him about your travels."

"Sounds exciting." Caitlin smiled up at the older boys with a dreamy look in her eyes.

Sam shook his head and groaned quietly.

"You guys are brothers?" asked Derek.

"Yep," the younger one answered. "I'm Hudson, this is my older brother, Giff."

Sam eyed the two brothers curiously. Hudson still looked to be about Derek's age. Giff seemed two or three years older, maybe sixteen or seventeen.

"That's an interesting name, Giff," said Mrs. Murphy. "Is it a family name or just a nickname?"

Hudson laughed. "He gets that a lot."

Giff nodded. "It's true. It's short for Gifford."

Sam remembered his dad talking about an old New York Giants player and then TV announcer with that name. "Like the football player?"

Giff chuckled. "No, that would be cool, though. When your father's a park ranger, he names you after famous foresters. Gifford Pinchot was the first head of the

US Forest Service. He's famous for being an early pioneer in the conservation movement along with Teddy Roosevelt."

"Teddy Roosevelt?" Derek's eyes opened wide. "That's pretty cool."

Giff shrugged. "It's better than Pinchot, I guess."

Caitlin laughed. "Your dad must like history."

Giff winked at her. "Just a bit. I guess we couldn't help but pick it up over the years."

"That's okay," said Caitlin. "We love history, too."

"So you're only hiking part of the AT?" asked Derek, emphasizing "AT" like he'd said it hundreds of times and was an experienced hiker. "Not the whole thing?"

Hudson nodded. "Yeah, it runs twenty-two hundred miles from Georgia to Maine. We don't quite have that much time."

"Whoa." Derek whistled. "That's far."

"Takes several months to thru-hike the whole thing," agreed Giff.

"I had ideas about being a park ranger when I was younger," said Mr. Murphy.

Giff nodded. "Right on."

"You did, Daddy?"

"What happened?" asked Sam.

Mr. Murphy shrugged. "Sometimes you have to make a choice when the paths converge in your life. I had an opportunity as a photography intern with *National Geographic* coming out of school. It was hard to turn down, so I didn't."

Mrs. Murphy put her hand on her husband's shoulder and squeezed. "I'd say it worked out pretty well."

"I think working at a national park sounds exciting," exclaimed Caitlin, staring at Giff and Hudson like they were movie stars. "There're so many amazing experiences."

Sam raised his eyebrows skeptically. "Like what?"

"Think about it," Caitlin gushed. "Taking care of nature, studying animal habitats, teaching visitors about the environment, hiking, camping—what's not to like?"

Sam's mind started churning with objections. "Bugs, poison ivy, snowstorms, steep cliffs. Oh, and did I mention bears?"

Derek shook his head. "I thought it was wolves that had you scared now."

Sam nodded. "Good point. Those too." He turned to the hikers. "You ever see any wolves out on the trails?"

Hudson tilted his head and turned to his brother. "I don't think wolves live in the Blue Ridge Mountains, do they?"

"Not practically speaking. The red wolf is nearly extinct. Dad talked to that guy in the Fish and Wildlife Service who'd tagged a few in North Carolina, remember?"

Derek nudged Sam's arm. "See, that's a whole other state. There's nothing to worry about."

Giff gestured into the trees. "Of course, keep in mind that North Carolina's only a few miles southeast of here."

Derek covered his eyes with his hand. "Don't tell him that."

Sam tried to move the conversation away from talking about his fears. If there was even a chance of wolves living in this area, he'd rather not know. He stared over at a mural painted across the side of the trailer behind the store. "Trailtown USA," he read aloud. "Why do they call it that?"

"Several trail systems start or intersect in Damascus," Giff answered.

"More than just the Creeper and the Appalachian?" asked Sam.

Giff nodded. "There's a bike trail that goes from Virginia to Oregon, wildlife and bird watching trails, and even the Crooked Road Trail."

"Crooked road?" said Derek. "What's that?"

Mrs. Murphy held her finger up. "I think Ginny told me about that once. It's tied into the history of country music, if I recall."

As if on cue, a man and a woman began strumming on guitars on the other side of the clearing. "Oh, look at that," exclaimed Caitlin.

"Maybe you should join them?" suggested her dad.

Caitlin shook her head quickly. "I don't even have my guitar, Daddy."

Hudson smiled. "You're a musician?"

Caitlin blushed. "No, not really. I'm just learning. Writing a few songs."

"I'm surprised she didn't bring her guitar along on the

bike trail," Derek moaned. "She played it nearly the whole way down on the drive from Richmond."

"That's cool," said Hudson. "I wish I could play."

Sam leaned back from the table and checked on their bikes. It was interesting talking to these guys, but he was tiring of watching Caitlin get all googly eyed as Hudson complimented her about her music. "We should probably get back on the trail, no?"

Derek smirked when he saw Sam's discomfort.

"You're probably right," said Mr. Murphy. "We told Ginny we'd meet her for dinner at The Tavern tonight at six. We're not too far from Damascus, but we still need to take the shuttle back to Abingdon."

"How much farther will you two hike today?" Mrs. Murphy asked the brothers.

Giff glanced at his watch and shrugged. "We'll see how it goes. I think it's about ten miles to the next shelter. But Hudson likes to take a little nap after lunch sometimes."

"Me?" Hudson frowned. "More like the other way around, bro." He waved as they stood from the table. "Nice meeting you all. Enjoy the rest of your ride." He smiled at Caitlin. "Keep working on your songs. Maybe I'll hear one on the radio sometime."

Sam chuckled louder than he intended, and Caitlin gave him a nasty look. He held his hand up apologetically. "Sorry."

"Those guys were cool," said Derek, as they climbed back on their bikes. "Maybe we could do that sometime,

Sam. You know, two bros, hiking the trail, living off the land, braving the wild… it could be great."

Caitlin laughed from behind them. "I can't quite picture the two of you getting along like that."

Sam nodded in agreement. "It does sound fun, all except the part about you being there."

Derek acted insulted. "Yeah, maybe you're right. But those guys seem to handle it. They should write a book series about their adventures. I'd certainly read it."

CHAPTER ELEVEN

The last few miles into Damascus went quickly, and after they returned their bikes to the shop, they were shuttled back to The Martha.

"That was really fun," said Caitlin as they climbed out of the van.

"Yeah, thanks for taking us," agreed Sam.

"Maybe we should turn around and do it again?" Derek pointed back to the road. "The western trailhead actually starts in Abingdon…"

Mrs. Murphy let out a cackle. "I think once will be enough for today. Those bike seats weren't as comfortable as I remember them."

"I think I might go relax for a while." Mr. Murphy nodded at the hotel's front porch. "One of those rocking chairs is calling my name."

Mrs. Murphy glanced toward Main Street. "But first,

there's a few shops and a bookstore I wanted to peek in…"

"Or we could do that." Her husband rolled his eyes. "See you kids in a few hours."

Mrs. Murphy frowned playfully. "Oh, stop."

"We need to explore the rest of the town, too," Caitlin said to the boys. "I mean, unless you guys want to nap or go along to the bookstore?"

Derek made a face. "No need to twist my arm. You had me at explore."

Mrs. Murphy motioned to them. "Remember, we're going to dinner tonight with Ginny at six. Stay together in town, okay?"

"We will," Caitlin called as they hurried down the driveway toward Main Street. The tree-covered brick sidewalk was lined with historic-looking buildings on all sides. Just past the Barter, they crested a hill and waited on the corner for the light to change. A square brick building was under construction across the street and a white sign proclaimed *Financed by WHI*.

"That Bernard guy seems to be everywhere," said Sam.

"No kidding." Caitlin pointed at the dark woodgrain doorway to their right. A gold-colored plaque was fitted into the brick. *Wolf Hills Investments*. "This must be his office. Maybe we should go in and make sure he's taking good care of Aunt Ginny."

Derek stared at the building curiously. "Good idea, let's check things out."

"What are you going to do?" asked Sam. "Walk into their office and ask for a financial evaluation?"

His brother grinned back at him. "Even better. Come on!" He turned the corner of the building, Sam and Caitlin following him to a door in the back. Derek walked up two brick steps and tried the knob. "It's locked."

"Did I say financial evaluation?" asked Sam. "I meant psychological evaluation."

Derek ignored him and moved to stand under a tall window beside the steps. A buzz sounded from Caitlin's pocket. "Shh," Derek motioned quickly. "Keep that quiet."

"It's from Aunt Ginny," Caitlin whispered, glancing at the screen. "She says Jake is still in the hospital. He has two bruised ribs, a leg fracture, and a concussion."

Sam grimaced at the news. "Ouch. He's going to be there for a few days, I'll bet."

"Well, let's see what old Bernard is up to." Derek placed a foot against the brick foundation. "Give me a boost. Maybe I can see if he's inside."

Sam scanned the quiet alley, but no one seemed to be around. He didn't know how they'd explain themselves if someone spotted them looking in windows. "What if someone sees us?"

"I'll be quick. I just need to get a foothold on this brick up here. If you hurry up and boost me, that is." They pushed Derek's foot higher until he grabbed the edge of the windowsill and steadied himself.

"Well?" called Sam. "What do you see?"

"I think that's Bernard. And he's talking with some other guy."

"Who is it?" asked Caitlin.

"Do they see you?" Sam groaned as he struggled to keep Derek boosted. Either his brother was in the middle of a growth spurt, or he was eating even more waffles than Sam.

"I don't think so." Derek strained to get higher. "His back is to the window. Wait, he's turning around…"

"Hey! What do you three think you're doing?" a gruff voice called from the other end of the alley. Sam glanced up and saw a man wearing a yellow hard hat and a tool belt staring at them.

Derek's weight shifted awkwardly, and he lost his balance. He tumbled to the pavement, but bounced up quickly. He smiled and brushed off his pants. "Oh, hi."

"I said, what are you three doing back here?" the construction worker repeated, his hands on his hips.

Derek held his palms up innocently. "Sorry, we were just looking for my brother's pet parakeet. We thought it flew in this window here."

Sam tried to keep a straight face as the man stared at him. "It's true… his name is… Perry."

The man looked at the building and then back at them. "That window's closed."

Derek shook his head. "I know. I can't figure out how he did it. I think he was standing on the ledge looking at his reflection or something. He's a very vain bird."

"Maybe somebody closed it after him," suggested Caitlin, holding back a giggle.

The worker lowered his eyebrows but motioned toward the road. "Maybe you three need to get moving before I call the cops."

Derek nodded. "Not a problem. Sorry to bother you, sir." He waved the rest of them toward the street as he made a whistling sound. "Perry! Here, Perry!"

When they were out of sight from the construction worker, Sam stopped and stared at his brother. "A parakeet?"

Derek shrugged. "I had to come up with something."

"And you picked that? I've never even had a parakeet."

"It worked, didn't it?"

"I guess."

Caitlin waved them off. "Enough with the parakeet. What else did you see through the window?"

Derek's face turned serious. "Bernard was meeting with some creepy-looking guy."

"Did you recognize him?" asked Caitlin.

"No. I've never seen him before."

Sam leaned against a tree and considered the possibilities. "It could easily just have been a normal meeting." It was Bernard Hostetter's office, after all. Then he had an idea. "Remember what we heard through the vent last night? That guy said he was going to meet someone tomorrow. Maybe we heard the guy Bernard was meeting with."

"Aunt Ginny did say Bernard was angry about not getting a controlling share of the theater," Caitlin replied.

"What if they purposefully tried to shut down the show to put the theater out of business?" said Derek. "Then Bernard could buy the whole thing on the cheap."

Caitlin twirled a strand of her hair as she considered Derek's idea. "It's not the craziest theory."

Sam held out his hands. "But if he owned the theater, wouldn't he want it to stay in business? You know, so it would make more money."

"That's what we'll need to figure out," said Caitlin.

"At least we have suspects," said Derek excitedly.

Sam wasn't so sure. "I think we need to keep narrowing it down. It could still be anybody."

"Come on, Sam." Derek folded his arms. "Haven't you ever watched any true crime shows?"

"No, have you?"

"Well… just that one time with Grandma. It was the one with the nosy old lady who wrote about all the mysteries she solved."

Caitlin looked up at him. "*Murder She Wrote*?"

"Yeah, I think so."

Sam shook his head. "We don't have a murder, Derek. And that wasn't a true crime show."

"Not yet we don't, but who knows what will happen next in this crazy town?"

They started walking toward The Martha when a heavy door closed behind them. They looked back and saw a man walking out of the WHI building. Derek pulled Sam and Caitlin behind a delivery truck parked at the curb. "Quick, get behind here."

Sam peered out from behind the truck and watched a man in front of the building stare into his phone. He was tall, well over six feet, and reminded Sam of someone trying to impersonate Abraham Lincoln, except without a top hat. He had a trimmed beard and wore a dark, expensive-looking suit.

"That's the creepy guy," whispered Derek.

Sam didn't remember seeing him before either. "Who do you think it is?"

Derek put his finger to his lips.

As they watched, Bernard also stepped out of the building. He called to the tall man and then handed him an envelope without speaking and went back inside the building. Creepy Abe Lincoln took the envelope and walked to a black BMW parked several spaces up the street. He slid behind the wheel and pulled away.

When the car was out of sight, the kids moved back to the sidewalk. "I don't like the looks of that guy," muttered Sam. "He's creepy."

Derek raised his eyebrows. "The Virginia Creeper. I told you it was a killer."

"Nobody's a killer, Derek." Caitlin glanced up the now empty street, although she didn't look too convinced.

"Did you see that envelope Bernard handed him?" asked Sam.

"It looked thick," said Derek. "Like it was stuffed with cash. A lot of it."

Sam looked at his brother over the rim of his glasses that had slipped low on his nose. "How do you know it was cash? It could be anything."

"Oh, yeah? What else could it have been, Sam?"

Sam tried to come up with something that made sense, but instead he blurted out the first thing he could think of. "Coupons?"

Derek bent over laughing. "You think Bernard is clipping coupons for savings on groceries? Geez, Sam."

Caitlin giggled. "Aunt Ginny said he's the richest guy in town. I think cash is a lot more likely."

"It's the payoff," said Derek. "It has to be."

Sam tilted his head. "Payoff?"

"Do I have to spell it out for you, Sam?" Derek folded his arms and sighed. "Think about it. Bernard hired the Creeper guy to take care of Greensboro in the play, and we just witnessed the payoff. It has to be."

Sam shook his head. "It has to be?"

Derek shrugged. "Okay, well, it doesn't have to be. But I think it *could* be."

Sam noticed Caitlin was quietly twirling a strand of hair with her finger again. She always did that when she was concentrating. "Well?"

She looked up at him in surprise. "Well, what?"

"Do you think it was a payoff, too?"

"I don't know. But they do seem suspicious. We need

more clues. Maybe Aunt Ginny can tell us more at dinner."

Derek stopped in the middle of the sidewalk and pointed up the street. "You might not have to wait until dinner. Isn't that her?"

Sam and Caitlin looked at where Derek was pointing up ahead. "Where?"

"Right there, just before the Barter."

Sam glimpsed someone walking up the steps by the theater lobby before they moved out of sight.

"Aunt Ginny!" Caitlin called. "Come on, maybe we can catch up to her."

CHAPTER TWELVE

When they reached the theater, the front door to the lobby was locked. Sam put his face up to the glass and tried to see inside. "Everything's dark. Are you sure it was her?"

Derek nodded. "Positive."

Caitlin pointed back to the sidewalk. "Maybe there's a side door. She must have stopped by to do some work before dinner. She could be backstage or in her office."

They walked around the alley to the right side of the building. The back looked like any normal warehouse with a large raised loading bay and two white doors.

Caitlin pointed to a long beam with a pulley that stuck out from the bricks above the doors. "That must be how they bring in the set pieces," said Caitlin. "Like the ones that fell on top of Jake."

Derek's head swiveled from the building to the trees

on the other side of the driveway. "If we can find a rope, maybe I could swing into that door from the trees…"

Sam pointed to a smaller door along the sloped driveway. "How about you just try that one, Tarzan?"

"You're so boring, Sam." Derek pressed himself up against the wall and slid toward the door dramatically. The handle turned and he pushed the door forward. "Jackpot."

"Hello? Aunt Ginny?" Caitlin called as they entered a windowless hallway.

Sam squinted in the darkness when the exterior door closed behind them. He tapped on his phone flashlight and tried to get his bearings. The long hallway had rooms on both sides. When he noticed the star on the outside of a door up ahead, he realized where they were. "That's Jake's dressing room."

Caitlin pointed ahead. "That means we have to go up these stairs to get to the stage."

Sam shined his light along a wall lined with framed photographs. Group shots like the kind for class pictures in elementary school. There were dozens of them, some in black and white with dates going back to the Barter's earliest days. Sam moved along the wall, staring at the frozen moments in time of all the different actors from over the years. "I wonder if Jake's in any of these?"

"That would have been back in the nineties, I think." Caitlin stepped slowly along the rows next to him. "This is about right." They both scanned the rows of faces. It was hard to pick people out with the flashlight's glare. Each individual in the big group shots was fairly small.

Sam leaned closer until a familiar face caught his eye. "Is that him?"

Caitlin moved next to him. "I think so. Wow, he's definitely young, but that would make sense." She read the date at the bottom. "1998. He's handsome."

"Uh-oh, Sam." Derek slipped behind them and chuckled. "Looks like you have a little competition. First the hikers and now a famous movie star. I don't think you stand a chance."

Sam shook his head. He glanced at Caitlin to see if she looked embarrassed, but she acted like she hadn't even noticed Derek's stupid joke.

"Who does that look like to you?" she asked, still staring at the picture.

Sam tilted his head. "Didn't we just say it was Jake?"

"No, right next to him." Caitlin put her finger on the glass. "Her."

Sam stared at a woman who looked like she was about college age. His eyebrows raised in recognition. "Is that your mom?"

"No…" Caitlin shook her head. "It's Aunt Ginny."

Derek pushed between them to see the picture. The woman had her head on Jacob Greensboro's shoulder. "Whoa, were they, like, an item?"

Caitlin stepped back from the wall. "I don't know, but they certainly look like it."

Sam tried to think about what that could mean. "Did she work at the Barter the same time as Jake?"

"Looks that way," Derek answered.

"Why wouldn't she have told us that?" asked Caitlin.

"Maybe everyone else knows," suggested Derek. "And they just didn't tell *you.*"

Sam watched Caitlin wriggle her nose. She always wanted to be the first to know things, and this was even worse if it involved her aunt. "Seems like something my parents would have mentioned when we were on our way here. It's not like them to keep secrets."

"Maybe they didn't know either," said Sam. "But it's not a bad thing, is it? They could have just been dating. It was a long time ago."

Caitlin bit her lip. "Maybe."

"We can ask her about it at dinner." Sam shined his light up the hallway. "Or we can ask her now, if she's still here."

"Hang on." Derek held up his hand for him to stay quiet. "Before we try to find her, we need to snoop around. Maybe we can find some clues about the accident." He opened the door on the other side of the hall marked *Trap Room.*

"What's in there?" asked Sam. Whatever the Trap Room was, it didn't sound very safe.

"Just come on."

They followed Derek into a small room with a hole up in the ceiling. Sam realized they were directly under the stage. The opening above them was the trap door used to get actors to appear or disappear through the floor. Derek climbed up a small scaffold and motioned for them to follow.

"Why don't we just go up the regular stairs?" asked Sam.

"Because this is way cooler, obviously." He stuck his head through the hole in the ceiling. "Woah…"

"Do you see Aunt Ginny?" called Caitlin.

"No, everything's pretty dark. Come up here, you guys."

Sam couldn't help himself and moved past Caitlin to the scaffold. "Let me see." He climbed through the hole and then reached back down and helped Caitlin. Suddenly, all three of them were standing on center stage.

"Pretty cool trick, huh?" marveled Derek.

Sam stepped to the edge of the stage and stared across the empty theater. Even though the lights were off, he could make out the rows of empty seats that looked even more red than normal under the gleam of the Exit signs.

He spied a bare bulb on the other side of the stage. He caught his breath, realizing it was just as Alexi had described.

Caitlin seemed to notice at the same time. "The ghost light."

Sam took a long breath and casually glanced up at the balcony.

Derek chuckled and tapped his arm. "There's not really a ghost up there, Sam."

"Oh yeah, then what did I see?"

"Beats me." Derek walked across the stage and stretched his hands out wide and bent at the waist into a dramatic bow. "To be a chicken, or not to be a chicken, that is Sam's question."

Sam walked into the wings of the stage and tried to ignore his brother's babbling to an imaginary audience. He shined his flashlight along the edge of the curtains and the ropes running to the ceiling. A wide assortment of set pieces, rolling tables and chairs, and racks of costumes were scattered about. He spotted the wooden backdrop of Red Riding Hood's grandmother's house moved off to the side. Sam pushed against it, but it didn't budge. It was no wonder it hurt Jake so badly when it fell on him.

Caitlin walked up next to him. "I don't think Aunt Ginny's here. We should probably leave. She wouldn't want us wandering around by ourselves." She pointed to the hall. "We can take the stairs this time."

At the bottom of the stairway, Derek pointed to another door along the hall. "Look, the Wardrobe Room. Didn't your aunt say that was where the tunnel was?"

Sam took a long breath. "She also said she didn't want to go anywhere near it." That whole idea gave him the creeps just thinking about it.

Derek ignored him and walked through the doorway. He flipped on the lights to reveal a cluttered room filled with shelves of just about everything. There were bins of material, sewing machines, an industrial washer and dryer, racks of clothes, laundry baskets, shelves of cleaning supplies, and even a portable spotlight and other extra equipment. Sam never thought about all the extra stuff that was required to put on a theater production at a place like the Barter. No wonder Ginny seemed busy all the time.

"Look, I think this is Aunt Ginny's desk." Caitlin leaned over a wide table on the other side of the room.

"Doesn't look much like a desk to me," said Derek.

"This is an old building," answered Caitlin. "They probably have to use whatever space they can find." She shuffled through several piles of papers and envelopes.

"Anything interesting?" asked Sam.

"Mostly bills and financial statements. I think the theater might really be in debt. Remember how she said they had to sell some ownership shares to Bernard?"

Derek walked over and glanced at the wall behind the desk. "See any more pictures of her and Jake? Or maybe a threatening letter that hasn't been sent yet?"

Caitlin swatted Derek's arm with an envelope. "Don't say that. Aunt Ginny didn't send the letter. That's ridiculous."

Derek stood straight and looked at her skeptically. "Is it? Or does it make so much sense that it's just blowing your mind?"

Sam shook his head. "I think you blew your mind a long time ago. Why would your aunt send Jake a threatening letter?"

Derek shrugged. "Who knows? There are lots of reasons."

"There's no way," said Caitlin. "But I'm going to ask my mom about their relationship when we see her. I'm surprised she's never said anything."

A door slammed somewhere in the building, echoing through the deserted hallways.

"What was that?" asked Sam.

Derek moved to the doorway and listened in the hallway. He spun around and scanned the room. "Someone's coming. We have to hide."

"Hide?" asked Sam. "Why?"

"What if it's Aunt Ginny?" asked Caitlin.

Derek's eyes widened. "Especially if it's her. She could be our main suspect. But even if it's someone else, they won't be happy that we're in here alone."

Now Sam could hear the tapping of shoes along the tile floor down the stairway. Someone was definitely coming in their direction.

"Quick, get inside that closet." Derek switched off the light and pointed his flashlight to a space near the concrete floor to the left of the shelves. A square, metal door with a gold-colored handle was built into the gray, stone wall.

Sam shook his head. "I'm not going in there."

Derek yanked the door open and a rush of cold air filled the room like he'd just opened a freezer. Chill bumps swept over Sam's arm.

"Yes, you are." Derek grabbed Sam's hand and pulled him through the opening. Caitlin squeezed next to them into the cramped space. They crouched together against a cold, stone floor as Derek pulled the door mostly closed, leaving it open just a crack so they could see out.

"It's freezing in here," moaned Sam. "I don't even know why we're hiding."

"Guys," whispered Caitlin. "This isn't a closet."

"What is it?" asked Derek. "One of those ice house refrigerators, like at Mount Vernon?"

Sam thought he could hear Caitlin gulp in the silence before she answered.

"It's the tunnel."

Sam tried to spring from his crouch back into the room, but Derek pushed him back down. "Someone's coming."

A sliver of light shot through the slightly open door as the lights came on in the wardrobe room. Sam strained to catch a glimpse, but the angles were wrong in the tight space. Suddenly, music started playing, and at first, he thought someone had turned on a radio. But he recognized the song. It was the ringtone he'd heard at breakfast.

Derek nodded ominously and mouthed silent words. "Ginny."

"Hello?" Ginny's voice sounded from out in the wardrobe room. They waited in silence to hear more of the conversation. Sam still didn't know why they were suddenly being so secretive. Sure, they'd seen Caitlin's aunt in the picture next to Jake, but what did that really mean?

"I told you, I need more time," Ginny answered. Sam

thought he sensed a hint of concern in the woman's voice. "I'm working on it, but the board has rules. I can't make all these big decisions on my own."

Sam pushed Derek's shoulder and squeezed closer to the crack in the door. His head scraped against the rock in the wall, but he could finally see. Ginny was rummaging around the desk table like she was looking for something.

"Yes, I understand. I said I'll do it, and I will. But I have to go now. Please stop calling me."

The conversation seemed to be over, but Ginny was still in the room. She dragged a chair across the floor, and Sam watched her climb up to reach high on a top shelf along the far wall. The chair wobbled as she stood on tiptoe, and, for a second, it looked like she was about to topple over. But then she steadied herself and pulled her arm back down.

Something was in her hand. Was it a bag? She climbed off the chair and set the object on the table, allowing Sam to see it clearly. He felt his stomach turn, and he leaned back from the door.

Suddenly, Ginny's footsteps walked closer. "What's that doing open?" she said aloud. She stood beside the door for several seconds, and Sam wondered if she had heard them breathing.

Then the door slammed shut with a thud.

It plunged them into darkness as the handle turned with a click and the sound of footsteps grew fainter till they left the room.

CHAPTER THIRTEEN

S am's heart pounded in his chest.

It was pitch black.

Derek pushed against the door, but it didn't budge. "I think she locked it."

"Why would she do that?"

"She didn't know we were in here," Caitlin whispered.

Sam leaned forward and banged on the door with his fist. "Help!"

"Quiet, someone will hear us." Derek flicked on his phone's light and shined it in Sam's face, blinding him.

"No kidding, I want to get out of here!" Sam blinked and tried to focus his eyes. The three of them were sitting on two stone steps which led up into darkness. The thick steps were a dirty mix of brown, gray, and black and sloped unevenly as though they had been carved by hand.

"I don't know what you think Aunt Ginny's doing, but we need to get out of this tunnel," said Caitlin.

Derek climbed to the top of the steps and stared out into the dark passage. "Didn't you hear her on the phone? Who do you think she's talking to, the dry cleaner? Or maybe she's swapping coupons too, like the Creeper."

"I don't care what you say. I'm getting out of here." Sam shouted and banged on the door a dozen times until his hand started to throb. He stopped and listened, but all was silent.

"She must have left right after she shut the door," said Caitlin.

Sam pulled out his phone and groaned when he saw the screen. "No service."

Derek patted the stone walls. "We're encased in solid rock. A signal won't reach under here."

Sam felt like throwing his phone at his brother. "Then how are we supposed to get out of here?"

"Oh, come on, it's not like there's a ghost in the tunnel." Derek moved the light under his chin. "Oh wait, they said there was one in here, too, didn't they?"

That was the last straw. Sam jumped up and lunged at his brother at the top of the stairs. His movement kicked up a cloud of gravel. Derek dodged Sam's attack and moved higher up the passage before sticking his tongue out at Sam in the shadows.

Caitlin coughed in the dust cloud and smacked Sam's leg. "Stop it, both of you! That won't help anything. Maybe we can work our way to the other end."

Sam sat on the cold stone and shook his head. "Ginny said the tunnel collapsed years ago, remember?"

Derek shined his light further ahead, but the ceiling was low, and the light was quickly swallowed up by the darkness. "We might as well try it and see. Sitting here isn't getting us anywhere."

Sam didn't feel like following his brother anywhere, but he also didn't want to be left alone. He sighed and climbed into the tunnel behind Derek and Caitlin, who were inching their way along the dirty passage on their knees. After a few yards, the ceiling moved higher and they could stand normally.

The chilly space gave him the creeps. "This is eerily familiar."

"There are no alligators down here, Sam."

"What about wolves?"

"Wolves don't live in basements."

"Neither do alligators. Or so we thought."

"Well, that was a unique situation."

"Uh-huh."

Caitlin stopped and turned toward Sam. "What was Aunt Ginny doing in the Wardrobe Room? All I could see was your head."

"She was climbing on a chair." Sam suddenly remembered what he'd seen. "And then she pulled something down from the top shelf."

"What was it?"

"An envelope."

Derek's mouth dropped open. "See! I told you she was the one who sent Jake that death threat. She was probably writing another one."

Sam shook his head. "No, not that kind of envelope. It was thick." He remembered the thought that crossed his mind when he saw it. "It was exactly like the one we saw Bernard give to the Creeper outside his office."

"A wad of cash?" asked Derek.

"It looked like it."

Caitlin frowned. "You don't know it was money. We don't even know what was in Bernard's envelope. Besides, why would she have so much cash?"

Derek folded his arms confidently. "It was a payoff."

"For what?" asked Caitlin.

"Could be anything. But if I had to bet, I'd say it was on its way to the Creeper for trying to axe Greensboro."

Sam gulped. That seemed unlikely, but the clues were adding up. "I don't know…"

"Aunt Ginny would never do that," Caitlin repeated.

"Who knows?" Derek replied. "But there seems to be more to Aunt Ginny than meets the eye."

Sam shined his light down the tunnel. "All I care about right now is getting out of here." They turned and continued along the passage, the walls narrowing so that they had to duck lower again. Sam kicked something along the floor that banged with a metallic clank.

"What was that?" asked Caitlin.

Sam bent down and brushed the dust off a metal box. It was an assortment of tools—a hammer, an old metal saw, screwdrivers—all just sitting there. But based on the amount of dust covering them, they'd been there for a long time. He picked up a wrench and held it in the light. "Why would anyone just leave this back here?"

Caitlin raised her eyebrows and glanced over at him. "Remember Ginny's story about the workers being scared off by spirits?"

Sam dropped the wrench back into the dirt. The last thing he needed to think about was whether there were lost spirits trapped in the tunnel. Not that he even believed in anything like that. "I don't know what they thought they saw down here, but I'm not sticking around to find out."

"Let's keep going," said Derek. He leaned under a half-finished wooden support brace and shined his light against the wall. "Look at this. That beam looks new compared to the others." He rubbed at a bolt with his fingers. "It's still shiny."

"But Ginny said it was decades ago that the workers were back here," said Caitlin.

Derek shrugged. "Well, somebody's been down here since."

Caitlin pointed ahead to piles of rubble that had been placed around the edges of the tunnel. "If this was the cave-in, it's fixed. Maybe we really can get through to the Barter."

Derek glanced at the stone ceiling just inches above his head. "We're probably under Main Street right now. All those cars driving right over top of us…." He tapped the stone and a cloud of dirt rained down on him.

Sam waited to make sure the tunnel didn't start

collapsing on them, but it held firm. He turned to walk forward but then froze. An icy chill swept over him, tussling his hair.

Derek glanced over at him. "Do you feel that?"

Sam looked at Caitlin to see if she'd sensed it as well, but given the look on her face, he didn't even have to ask. "How is that possible? We're underground."

"Maybe there's some kind of crevice or underground stream," Caitlin said and bit her lip.

Sam suddenly understood why the workers might have fled the tunnel years ago. There was a creepy feeling down here that was hard to explain. He didn't have any tools, but if he did, he'd probably have dropped them, too.

"Let's get out of here!" called Derek, hurrying forward. Caitlin stumbled over an uneven part of the gravel floor, but she kept her balance and kept moving. They didn't stop running until they reached a wall. Sam bent forward and rested with his hands on his knees, catching his breath. He stared up at the wall and wondered if it was a dead end. He wasn't sure he could go back through the tunnel again.

Derek panned his light around the shadows and revealed a door. "Look at that! This has to be The Martha."

Sam hoped he was right, but what was the chance that it was unlocked, or even useable after all this time? Derek pushed at the handle, but it didn't budge.

"What if they sealed it off?" asked Caitlin.

"Sealed it off?" Derek put his hands on his hips like he was a construction manager. "What does that even mean?"

Sam shook his head. "It means they made sure it won't open, dummy. They probably didn't want anyone getting stuck here by mistake."

Derek waved his hand. "Sounds more like they just don't want anyone exploring."

Sam stared at his brother incredulously. "I can't imagine who would get an idea to do something like that."

"I think we just need to push," said Derek, pressing his weight against the door.

"Why don't we try banging?" asked Sam. "Maybe someone will hear us."

"We tried that on the other end, in the theater, if you remember," replied Derek. "It didn't work out very well."

"That was because the theater was empty and no one was around," said Caitlin. "If this door really leads to The Martha, there's lots of people in the hotel. Maybe somebody will hear us."

Derek lifted his hands and stepped back. "Be my guest."

Sam and Caitlin pounded on the door and yelled at the top of their lungs for close to a minute. Sam felt the energy draining from him as exhaustion mixed in with his panic. They stopped and listened, and then tried again, but just like the other door, there was only silence.

A bead of sweat rolled down Sam's forehead. What if

there was nothing behind that door but dirt? What if it didn't even lead to The Martha? They could be stuck down here forever!

"You finished?" asked Derek.

Sam sank to the floor. His throat was dry and now his hand hurt again from the pounding. "I guess."

Derek moved back to the door. "I think we need to ram it."

"With what?" asked Caitlin.

"With our shoulders."

"That's a good way to break a shoulder," Sam muttered from the ground, flexing his fingers to get normal feeling back in them.

"Yeah?" asked Derek. "How's your hand feeling right about now? Didn't work out so well either, did it?"

Sam folded his arms. "Fine. Ram the wall. What do I care?"

Derek grinned. "Okay, now we're talking. Give me some room." He hopped up and down and stretched like he was about to attempt a thousand-pound deadlift or some other Herculean feat. He moved a couple of yards from the door and lowered to a sprinter's stance.

"One, two, three!" He took three fast strides and barreled into the door.

Except he didn't hit it.

Just as his shoulder and the door were about to collide, the door groaned and jerked open. But Derek was moving too fast. He didn't have time to hit the brakes. He burst through the opening, arms flailing wildly. He tried to stop himself, but instead, crashed smack into Oliver, The Martha's front desk clerk.

Sam wished he could have captured a picture of the man's expression as Derek hit him like a linebacker. They tumbled into the hallway and banged against a table on the far wall. A flower vase fell to the ground and shattered.

For a moment, neither Derek nor Oliver moved. Sam worried that they'd knocked each other unconscious, but finally Derek rolled over and rose to his feet.

Oliver groaned and looked up at them. He took Derek's outstretched hand and stood. "What in the world was that?"

"You opened the door," said Derek.

"Yes, I know that. I'm the one who opened it. Why did you tackle me? And what are you three doing in there?"

Caitlin stepped forward. "We're sorry. We were accidentally locked in at the other side of the tunnel. No one in the Barter was there to let us out, so we crossed to this side."

Oliver looked skeptical. "This passage has been closed off for years. I didn't even know this door was functional until I heard your banging on the other side."

"Looks like it works to me," said Derek.

Oliver leaned through the open door and shivered in the darkness. "I don't even want to know what's in there. I've heard too many stories. They don't pay me enough to deal with this kind of stuff. No wonder they're talking about selling this place."

Caitlin raised her eyebrows. "What do you mean, selling? The Martha?"

The man suddenly looked nervous. "Nothing. I mean… oh, what does it matter, really? I'm leaving at the end of the summer for grad school in South Carolina." He leaned toward them and lowered his voice. "I overheard the owner talking about selling to some investment company. I don't know the details, but there've been some heated emails about it in the administrator's account." He glanced down the hall and then back at them. "Not that I've been reading them, of course. That's just what I've heard."

Caitlin shook her head. "Oh, no."

Oliver shrugged. "I'm sure the hotel will be fine." He checked his watch and then nodded to them. "Run off to your parents now. I don't want to see any of you near here again, understood? If the owner finds out you were in there, it could mean my job. I may be leaving, but I need this month's pay for my tuition."

CHAPTER FOURTEEN

"Well, that was interesting," said Derek, staring back at the inn from the gazebo on the front lawn.

"Just promise me we won't go back into that tunnel." Sam leaned against the wooden bench, the sunshine warm on his skin. They needed some time to debrief, and it felt great to breathe fresh air. He tried to walk himself step by step through everything that had happened—the accident at the theater, the mysterious conversation through the vent, the tall man with Bernard, Ginny's phone call, the envelope, the spooky tunnel, talk of the inn being sold—it was getting hard to keep track of it all.

Caitlin seemed to feel the same way. She tucked her legs underneath her in the seat next to him in the gazebo and chewed on a loose strand of her hair. "I keep thinking we're missing something."

"What if it's all connected?" called Derek as he

walked over to the fruit tree next to the gazebo. He picked up three fallen crabapples and tried to juggle.

Sam shaded his eyes and looked at his brother. "What do you mean?"

"Ginny, Bernard and the Creeper, and even Jake's accident." Derek got the apples moving in rhythm for a second or two, but then they fell to the ground. "What if they're all related to each other?"

Caitlin shook her head. "I told you. Aunt Ginny had nothing to do with the accident at the Barter. She loves the theater. Why would she sabotage it?"

"Don't forget the picture of her and Greensboro," said Derek. "She's hiding something. I can feel it."

Sam nudged Caitlin's side. "Are those your parents up there on the porch?"

She turned and glanced up at the line of white rocking chairs and loungers. When her mom waved down at them, Caitlin stood and grabbed Sam's arm. "Come on, I need your support."

"For what?"

"We have to talk to my mom about Aunt Ginny. Maybe she knows something about what happened."

They walked past Derek just as an apple smacked him in the nose. "I think I'll stay here and keep working at this," he moaned.

Caitlin's parents were lounging on two oversized wicker chairs with thick, floral-patterned cushions. Mr. Murphy seemed to be asleep while Mrs. Murphy read a book. She glanced up as they approached and set the book in her lap. "I thought that was you three down there. Isn't the breeze just heavenly? I could sit here all day."

Caitlin nodded toward her dad. "Looks like the bookstore was too much for him."

Mrs. Murphy chuckled. "You know your father. He could fall asleep in the middle of a rock concert if he wanted to." She pointed to the open chairs across from them. "Have a seat. What have you been up to?"

Sam felt his pulse quicken just thinking about sneaking around the theater and getting trapped in the tunnel. He didn't know where to begin.

"Oh, just exploring around the town," Caitlin answered quickly.

They sat in the open chairs facing the lawn and Main Street. Mrs. Murphy was right. It was a relaxing spot. But Caitlin was squirming in her seat.

Sam knew she didn't enjoy pressing her mom for information. Maybe this was what she needed his support with. He turned to Mrs. Murphy and tried to think of a good way to get the conversation started. "How long has your sister lived in Abingdon?"

He watched Caitlin breathe and nod him a thank-you.

"Oh, a long time," Mrs. Murphy answered. "She came here right after college and never seemed to want to leave. She was out of the house by the time I went to school in Williamsburg."

"Were you close growing up?" Sam asked.

"Why sure, we're sisters."

Sam thought about how Caitlin often made a big deal about being an only child. She seemed to like hanging out with Sam and Derek together, despite Derek's antics.

"Even back then?" asked Caitlin.

"We drifted for a while after she left home, but you know how much we talk now."

Caitlin glanced at Sam and chuckled. "A lot."

Sam tried to think of how to get at the information they wanted without being too obvious. "She never got married?"

Mrs. Murphy sighed, like it was something she'd thought about often. "No, she's had a few serious relationships, but they didn't work out. She's had a tough time with love, I'm afraid."

"What about here at the theater?" asked Caitlin. "Has she ever dated anyone?"

"Like an actor, maybe?" added Sam.

"Girl, if you twirl that hair any tighter, you might just spin away like a top." Mr. Murphy looked over at them with one eye closed. Apparently, he wasn't sleeping after all. "What are you two getting at?"

Caitlin self-consciously stopped fooling with her hair and sat up straight. "Well, it's just that we've been investigating the accident, you know, and—"

"You mean you've been snooping," said Mr. Murphy. "I thought we'd talked about how that usually gets you three in trouble." He stretched and sat up in his seat. He reached over and squeezed his wife's hand. "You might as well tell them. At this rate, there's no telling what conspiracy theory they might stumble on."

"Conspiracy theory?" asked Sam.

Mr. Murphy chuckled. "I mean, you three have noses like bloodhounds for digging up trouble. Even if there's none to be found." He shook his head. "I've never seen anything like it."

Sam watched the expression on Caitlin's mom's face. He couldn't tell if it was worry or frustration, but after a moment, her eyes softened. "How did you find out?"

"We saw a picture in the theater. Actually, Sam did. Aunt Ginny was standing next to Jake in a group shot of an old production. Her head was on his shoulder."

"I thought it was you, at first," said Sam.

Mrs. Murphy laughed. She reached out and ran her fingers through Caitlin's hair. "Ginny didn't come home that summer after her first year of college. My parents were afraid she'd run off with the circus or something. Grandpa said he thought she'd turned into a gypsy, but in reality, she'd joined on with the theater company here in Abingdon. She and Jake met working on a production of *Romeo and Juliet*, and that was all she wrote, as they say."

"They started dating?" asked Sam.

Mrs. Murphy nodded. "She fell for him hard. And no wonder. He was a few years older than her, but so tall and handsome. I'm not surprised he turned out to be such a big movie star. He was new to acting, and outside of this little town, no one had ever heard of him."

"So they were in love?" asked Caitlin.

"Desperately. We started hearing less and less from her until she finally wrote a letter. She explained how a Hollywood producer had seen Jake perform at the Barter. He'd offered him a role in a movie out in LA, and she was going with him."

"Was it *Panama Conspiracy*?" gasped Sam. He knew that was one of Jake's early Clint Patterson movies, but he didn't know if it was his first.

"Bingo," said Mr. Murphy.

"So what happened?" asked Caitlin. "Did Aunt Ginny move to Hollywood? I've never heard her mention that, either."

Mrs. Murphy shrugged. "She doesn't like to talk about it. Probably because it didn't last long. She followed Jake to the big city, and, as you know, that movie turned into a colossal hit. He was quickly caught up in the limelight and left poor Ginny on the curb, so to speak."

"He dumped her?" Caitlin seemed to take the news hard.

"Essentially," said Mrs. Murphy. "He took to life in the fast lane, and Ginny took a flight back to Abingdon. She started working at the theater while finishing her schooling on the side. But as far as I know, she never performed again on the stage. She decided to work on the production side of things after that."

"That's terrible," said Caitlin. "How could he do that to her?"

"Sometimes life takes us on different paths, honey. I don't know if he was trying to hurt her on purpose, but love, like lots of things in life, doesn't always go the way you think it will." Mrs. Murphy stared out at the lawn. "But like I told you before, Ginny's a big girl. She knows how to take care of herself. She pulled things together and has made a great life for herself here. Now she's the theater director. As far as I can tell, she's happy."

The cell phone on the table next to their chairs buzzed and made everyone jump. Mrs. Murphy laughed and looked down at the screen. "She must have heard us talking about her. That's Ginny now. Probably checking about dinner."

Caitlin stood and walked over to the railing. Sam joined her and gazed across the lawn. Derek had somehow gotten four apples in rotation at once, which was pretty impressive. A man walking past on the sidewalk said something to him. A wide grin filled Derek's face, but he quickly lost his balance. Everything crashed to the ground and two of the apples splattered on the concrete. He covered his face with his hands and then collapsed onto the grass as Sam and Caitlin laughed from the porch.

Caitlin glanced over her shoulder at her mom on the phone. "Can you believe that? Poor Aunt Ginny. I feel terrible for her."

Sam nodded, but something about the story wasn't sitting right in his mind. Caitlin must have noticed his expression. "What are you thinking?"

"I guess I'm surprised that she would want to work so closely with Jake again after all that had happened."

Caitlin closed her eyes. "Unless she was intentionally trying to get close to him again. Unless she had a plan to get even…"

Sam felt bad. He wasn't trying to hurt her feelings, but maybe Derek was right. Maybe everything was connected. Even Ginny.

CHAPTER FIFTEEN

"Look, it's Alexi." Caitlin pointed to the library window across the porch. The old man was sitting in the same spot where they'd seen him before.

"Does he just sit there all day?" asked Sam.

"I don't know, but we should say hi."

"Do we have to? He's kind of weird."

"I think he's nice." Caitlin tugged at Sam's arm and pulled him toward the front door.

When they entered the library, the old man looked up and smiled warmly, like he'd been watching them through the window and had been waiting for them to come in. "Ah, you have returned for our game of chess, correct?"

Sam rolled his eyes. It didn't seem like he was going to shake this guy. "Sure, why not?"

Derek followed them into the library and sat on the couch next to Caitlin. "Can I watch, too?"

Sam raised his eyebrows. "That doesn't seem like a good idea."

"We'll be quiet. We promise," said Caitlin. "Right, Derek?

"Like a mouse."

Sam would believe that when he saw it, but he sat down at the chessboard anyway.

"So, how has your day been?" Alexi asked as he arranged the pieces on the board.

"We rode bikes on the Creeper Trail," Sam answered. "And we had lunch in Damascus." As he said the words, it felt like those things had happened weeks ago.

Alexi nodded. "Beautiful area. So much to do. I've enjoyed it greatly over the years."

"Did you grow up in Abingdon?" asked Caitlin.

"No, I was born in Hungary, in a small village outside Budapest. My family emigrated when I was a teenager, not much older than you three. But that was a long time ago. I attended university in Blacksburg and then moved to Abingdon after graduation."

Sam hadn't expected such a long explanation. But it was pretty cool that the man had been born in Europe. "Do you still live here? Or are you staying at the hotel?" He didn't want to be nosy, but it seemed like the old man usually spent his entire day sitting in the library.

Alexi glanced out the window toward Main Street. "I thought I might retire here, once, but after my wife passed, I decided I needed a change of scenery. Too many memories. I live in Charlotte now."

"I'm so sorry," said Caitlin.

"Why? Charlotte is a delightful place." He chuckled at his joke.

Sam felt bad that he'd brought up a sensitive subject, but that still didn't clarify what the guy was doing here. "So, you're just visiting the hotel, then?"

"My son lives here. And I come often for business. He's been going through a rough patch with his family. But I like to see my grandchildren. There's two of them, a little younger than you all. A boy and a girl."

"You stay here?" asked Derek. "Why don't you stay at your son's house?"

Caitlin shot Derek a look like he was being rude, but the old man only chuckled as a bell jingled at the entrance door in the lobby. "We've found it works best when I stay here at The Martha. It gives us all a little space. And I find this old room comforting."

Sam glanced at Derek and wondered if their parents would be okay sending him to stay at a hotel sometimes. Some extra space sounded nice. As they talked, a man in a black T-shirt and jeans walked into the library. He looked about the same age as Sam's dad.

Alexi waved him over. "And here is my son now. We were just talking about you, Nicholas."

Nicholas nodded to everyone around the game table. "Hello, and it's Nick." He glanced at the chess set. "Still trying to hustle the guests, I see, Dad?"

Alexi made a face like he was offended. "Hustle? Of course not. Simply passing the time. You and I spent a fair number of evenings around one of these sets as well, if you remember."

Nick rolled his eyes. "How could I forget?" He glanced at his watch. "About ready to go? You promised to watch the kids tonight. Michelle is out of town and I'm working. Did you remember?"

"Of course." Alexi smiled and turned back to them. "See what I mean? They keep me young."

Nick looked at Caitlin curiously. "You're Ginny Moss's niece, aren't you?"

"Yes, do you know her?"

"I used to work at the theater when I was younger. We were in a few productions together. I ran into her at the grocery store last week and she mentioned you were coming. Plus, there aren't a lot of other girls your age who would sit around a chessboard with my father."

"Are you an actor?" asked Derek. "Is that why you worked at the theater?"

Nick chuckled. "Mostly just stage crew. I performed for a few years, but things didn't work out the way I'd planned, and eventually I gave it up and found something else to pay the bills. We all have to grow up sometime."

Alexi swatted at the air. "Don't let him fool you. He was very good. He just didn't stick with it long enough. His mind is always running off to try each new venture that catches his fancy."

Nick groaned and looked across the room. "That's not

what happened, Dad. The restaurant was a good idea. Everybody thought so."

"Yes? And now you're a glorified waiter who too often sleeps in the extra room above the bar."

"Who knew there was about to be a recession?" Nick shrugged. "How many times do I have to explain to you? I'm the general manager, Dad. I don't just tend bar. And it was just a couple times that I slept at the office. Michelle and I are working on things. Why can't you give me the benefit of the doubt sometimes?" He sighed in frustration and turned toward the lobby. "I'll be in the car. Come out when you're ready. Nice meeting you, kids."

An awkward silence filled the room for a few moments. Sam wished they hadn't been in the middle of such a personal conversation.

"I'm sorry you had to see that," Alexi said finally. "I love my son, but sometimes I get agitated. I have high expectations for him, but we both say too much. I need to learn to keep my mouth shut."

Sam glanced at Derek. "That happens in families."

The old man stood slowly from his wooden chair. "But I'm afraid it is now my turn to postpone our chess match."

Sam nodded and tried not to look relieved. "That's okay."

"Enjoy your time at The Martha," said Alexi. "I hope we see each other again before you head home."

"Enjoy watching your grandkids," said Caitlin as they watched Alexi follow his son out the door.

"That was awkward," said Derek.

Caitlin bit her lip. "Kind of sad, actually."

"But since it looks like there's an open seat…" Derek jumped from the couch and slid into the vacated chair across the table. "I'll take his spot."

"I don't think so." Sam rose quickly. "We've tried that before, and it never ends well."

"I'll play you," Caitlin volunteered, stepping next to Sam's chair.

Derek hesitated, but then nodded. "Okay, but I'll warn you now. I'm pretty good."

Caitlin's lips narrowed. "We'll see." She pointed at the pieces lined up on his side of the board. "White goes first."

Derek chuckled. "Even better." He slid a pawn forward two spaces.

Sam watched from the edge of the couch as Caitlin quickly moved one of her pawns up two spaces near the middle of the board as well.

"Stop copying me." Derek snorted. "I'm not sure if you know the rules, but if you don't, pawns can move one or two spaces to start."

Caitlin made a surprised face. "They can?"

Derek nodded and then moved another pawn near the middle of the board ahead one space. "Just to mix it up a little." He flashed a confident smile and seemed quite proud of himself.

Caitlin smiled back. "Right. That's smart." Then she calmly slid her queen on a diagonal to the side square. "Check."

Derek lowered his eyebrows. "What? A little early for that. I'll just move here." He placed his knight next to Caitlin's queen.

"Still check."

Caitlin didn't say anything else, but Sam thought her sly smile suggested something was up. He leaned closer to the board. "Wait, is that a checkmate?" He looked at Caitlin and then at his brother. "It is! Ha! She checkmated you in two moves!"

Derek stared at the board for a few more seconds, but he eventually realized that she'd trapped his king. There was nowhere to go. Caitlin had boxed him in perfectly.

He looked up at her in shock. "Okay, how'd you do that? Did you move a piece while I wasn't looking?"

Caitlin grinned. "No trick. It's a common move."

"Oh, yeah? What's it called?"

"Fool's Mate."

"And you're the fool, Derek!" Sam burst out laughing and began jumping around the room. "Wait until I tell Alexi that she beat you in two moves."

"I still think you cheated," argued Derek.

"We can play again if you want…"

Derek pushed back from the table in disgust. "Nah, I think that's enough for now. We've gotta get ready for dinner soon, anyway."

CHAPTER SIXTEEN

Caitlin was quiet on the walk from The Martha along Main Street to dinner. Telling her parents about everything they'd discovered would raise too many questions, and they didn't have any real answers. Not yet, at least. Sam glanced at the windows of Wolf Hills Investments as they walked past, but everything was dark. There was no sign of Bernard or The Creeper.

They continued down the slight hill toward a faded, gray, two-story building with white trim and black shutters. A dark shingled roof sloped sharply toward the street. A tall, stately wooden signpost rose from the curb. *The Tavern. Est. 1779.*

Derek whistled as they stopped in front of the building. "1779. Now that's old. Is this really where we're eating?"

Caitlin's dad nodded. "That's the plan."

Mrs. Murphy read from a page posted on a bulletin

board along the wall. "According to this, we're standing by the oldest historic building in town. And listen to all the famous guests who have stayed here over the centuries —Henry Clay, the king of France, Andrew Jackson—it's amazing!"

"You mean they've eaten here," said Derek. "Since it's a restaurant."

"Not necessarily, wise guy." Mrs. Murphy scanned lower on the page. "It's actually had quite a varied past. This building has functioned as a tavern and inn for stagecoach travelers, a bank, bakery, barber shop, post office—all kinds of things!"

Sam tried to imagine the old structure serving all those different purposes. He supposed over that much time, a place could do a lot. He walked past a window and noticed an odd rectangular hole. The building's exterior wasn't brick like most of the other old structures on the street. It had a plaster-like finish. "That's weird. It's like a brick fell out, except there's no bricks."

"It's the original mail slot."

Sam looked up at a woman in a white shirt who was clutching a stack of menus. "Really?"

"Sure is. This was the first post office on the western side of the Blue Ridge once upon a time. Believe it or not, we still get our mail through that slot each day."

"Wow," exclaimed Mrs. Murphy. "How amazing that such a little detail has survived."

"Food's good too." The woman grinned. "I'll bet

you're Murphy, party of six…" She did a quick head-count. "Or is it five?"

"That's us," answered Caitlin.

"We're still waiting for one, but she should be here soon," said Mrs. Murphy. Sam remembered that Ginny was coming to dinner as well.

"Well, I'm Tessa, and your table's ready, so why don't you follow me? I hope you brought your appetites." As she led them through the front doorway, it felt like someone had transported them back in time. The ceiling was low and supported by thick, dark wood beams which ran all the way to a stone wall and matched the deep windowsills. The floors in the entrance were brick, but the next room had wide, wooden boards under the tables.

"Wow, look at this place," muttered Mr. Murphy.

"Right here's the oldest bar in Virginia, and one of the oldest in the country." Tessa pointed to a rectangular wooden box that was built into the wall to their right. Several stools lined the front, and rows of bottles filled glass shelves along the back wall.

Derek made a goofy wave and acted like he was going to sit on a stool. "If you need me, I'll be here at the bar."

Mr. Murphy raised his eyebrows. "Nice try."

Derek held his hands up. "See, guys. I try to learn about history, but people keep holding me back."

A man in a black T-shirt moved behind the wooden counter from the next room. He glanced up and smiled. "Evening, folks."

"Hey, it's Nick!" exclaimed Derek.

Sam had remembered Alexi saying his son was a bartender, but he hadn't thought it might be at The Tavern.

"Nice to see you kids again. Are you here for dinner?"

Derek smacked the wood counter with his hand and spoke in a deep voice. "No, Nick, I'm here for a drink. Give me a Coke on the rocks, will ya? Actually, let's get crazy. Make it a Cherry Coke. No ice." He motioned to the others with a toothy grin. "And the same for all my friends, too."

"Yes, we're here for dinner." Mr. Murphy put his hand on Derek's shoulder and shook his head. "We're still trying to figure this one out."

Caitlin turned to her parents. "Nick knows Aunt Ginny. He used to work at the Barter."

"And you are clearly her much younger sister," replied Nick, looking at Mrs. Murphy.

Caitlin's mom just laughed. "Not too much younger, I'm afraid. But yes, Ginny's my sister. She's joining us for dinner tonight, but she's running a little late."

"I'll send her right through to your table when she comes in," said Nick. "Have a nice meal. I highly recommend the Wienerschnitzel."

"Wienerschnitzel?" Sam's face contorted.

Derek cracked up. "You should definitely have that, Sam."

Sam ignored his brother and looked back at Nick. "What is it?"

Nick chuckled. "Trust me. It's a traditional German dish, and it's very good."

They turned and followed Tessa through a room of tables and past a stone fireplace. They continued through a back door that opened up to an outdoor section. A dozen tables were scattered around a brick patio enclosed by a wooden fence. Sam looked up at white lights strung from the trees and noticed a long, wooden deck along the second floor with additional seating.

"Wow," marveled Caitlin. "It's like a secret garden. I didn't know this was back here."

Tessa directed them to a long table with a candle in the center.

"Isn't this nice?" Mrs. Murphy turned to the boys. "I think next time your parents should come along, too."

Sam nodded. "I think they'd like it."

Mrs. Murphy glanced at the back door. "Kids, I know we were talking about Ginny's past earlier, and you might have some questions, but I want you to be gentle with her. She's had a tough time with last night's accident. We need to support her as much as we can."

Derek started to say something, but Sam kicked him under the table. He'd shared back in their room what Caitlin's parents had told them about Ginny and Jake, but as much as the information had fueled their suspicions, there wasn't really any hard evidence against her. Maybe she really did feel uncomfortable about having her old flame back in town and it was just making her act peculiar.

Caitlin spotted her aunt standing with Nick at the back door, and she waved her over. Ginny pointed at them and walked over in a bustle.

"How are you coping, Ginny?" asked Mrs. Murphy.

Ginny threw her head back and breathed deeply. "If I can make it through this week, I can make it through anything. I was at the theater again this afternoon."

"Did something else go wrong?" asked Caitlin carefully.

"I heard from the detective regarding the incident."

Mrs. Murphy leaned forward. "And… what did he say?"

Ginny shook her head like she was almost afraid to get started. Sam couldn't tell if she was about to burst out laughing or fall into tears. "Well, he told me they've determined the rope that sent the sandbag flying into the set piece hadn't just frayed or broken from overuse. He said someone cut it with a knife."

"Oh my gosh," gasped Mrs. Murphy.

"You mean it was deliberate?" asked Caitlin.

Ginny closed her eyes. "Apparently so."

"It was just like the letter warned." Derek's eyes narrowed and he shot a knowing glance across the table at Sam and Caitlin. He looked like he was ready to shine a spotlight on Ginny right there at dinner and deliver a full interrogation, but he kept his mouth shut.

"But why would someone want to do that?" asked Mrs. Murphy.

"Your guess is as good as mine, but until we can

determine who did it or why it happened, they're closing us down," said Ginny.

"But the Barter is an institution," Caitlin exclaimed. "They can't shut it down."

"Do they have any leads?" asked Mr. Murphy.

Ginny shook her head. "Not that they've shared with me."

"We've been trying to narrow the suspects," said Derek.

Caitlin's parents exchanged glances across the table. "I don't know that you three should get in the middle of this."

Caitlin held out her hands. She looked like she couldn't hold it in any longer either. "How could we not, Mom? We're already in the middle of it."

"And besides," added Derek, "it's what we do."

Ginny stopped buttering her dinner roll and looked up warily. "What you do?"

"We solve mysteries," said Derek, a cocky grin on his face. Sam held his breath, unsure what his brother would say as he leaned closer to Ginny. "We think this one might involve a payoff. We saw someone meeting with the Virginia Creeper today."

"Virginia Creeper?" asked Mr. Murphy.

Derek grinned. "Yeah, that's what I'm calling him."

Ginny looked nervous. Or was she just confused? It was hard to tell. "What you're calling who?"

Derek's face turned serious. "I can't say yet for sure. We're still collecting evidence."

"Derek," said Mr. Murphy, "let's leave the detective work to the police, okay? We all want to relax and enjoy our dinner tonight."

Right then, Tessa floated over to the table to take their orders. The break in the conversation seemed to calm the mood, and Sam thought Mr. Murphy was right. It was probably best not to get deeper into things with Ginny during dinner.

After they ordered, Sam excused himself to wash his hands. He also wanted a reason to check out more of The Tavern's old rooms. It was fun to consider that travelers had been stopping at this place for centuries, some after hopping off a stagecoach rumbling into town along the cobblestones. Every corner he looked at made him think he was an extra in a scene from *Lord of the Rings,* or maybe *Narnia.*

A different server pointed Sam back toward the entrance for the restrooms. After washing and drying his hands at the sink, he stopped inside the door before walking back into the restaurant. He heard someone walk in from the street and start talking with Nick at the bar. The deep voice sounded familiar, but he couldn't place it.

Sam cracked open the restroom door. A tall man in a dark suit was arguing with Nick. Sam recognized him immediately. It was the Virginia Creeper! Then he remembered where he'd heard that deep voice. It was from the vent in Room 403!

Sam knew he had to get back to the table and tell Derek and Caitlin what he'd learned, but that would mean walking right past The Creeper. What were he and Nick arguing about? Sam tried to linger by the door and listen to what the men were saying, but a toilet flushed in one of the bathroom stalls. He had to move before someone came out and caught him eavesdropping.

He slipped out of the restroom door and made his way behind The Creeper at the bar and outside to the patio. Back at the table, Caitlin's parents were talking with Ginny about the local farmer's market. They seemed absorbed in their conversation, so Sam sat and gestured for Derek and Caitlin to slide closer.

"The vent voice is The Creeper," he whispered.

"What?" asked Derek.

Sam rolled his eyes and explained who he'd seen.

"Where was this?" said Caitlin.

"At the bar. He's arguing with Nick."

"Oh, so it's not okay for me to go to the bar, but for you, it's no problem?" Derek threw his head back. "How is that fair?"

Sam hushed him. "I wasn't at the bar. I just walked by it."

Caitlin looked toward the restaurant. "What were they arguing about?"

Sam tried to remember anything meaningful. "I couldn't really make out their conversation, but it was definitely the same guy. Nick seemed to know him, and he didn't seem happy."

Caitlin bit her lip. "That confirms it. If the Creeper is the same person as the voice in the vent, then he and

Bernard have to be involved in what happened to Jake at the theater. Now we just have to figure out why."

"We still need proof," said Sam. "We don't really have any evidence."

"Maybe this means Ginny is innocent after all." Caitlin looked over at her aunt and let out a long breath. "Still, we need some privacy to think this through."

"Why don't we head back to The Martha?" suggested Derek.

Sam felt his stomach rumble and glanced around the restaurant. "What about dinner? We haven't even eaten yet."

"After we eat," said Caitlin.

"Don't worry, Wienerschnitzel," said Derek. "You're not going to starve."

CHAPTER SEVENTEEN

Food had a way of taking Sam's mind off of trouble, and dinner at The Tavern was no exception. Despite Derek's teasing, Sam had taken Nick's suggestion and ordered the Wienerschnitzel. Once Mrs. Murphy explained what it was, that is. Nick hadn't lied—the breaded veal cutlet with mushroom sauce was delicious.

The grown-ups seemed happy to sit outside and keep chatting, so Caitlin talked her parents into letting them be excused after promising to walk straight back to The Martha. When they reached the entrance back into the restaurant, Nick was loading stacks of dirty glasses into the dishwasher. There was no sign of the Creeper.

"Looks like he left." Sam turned toward the front door, but then realized Derek was still standing in front of the long wooden bar. Not again.

"Hey, Nick!" Derek leaned over the counter so he

could see the man moving things around in the lower cabinets.

Nick's head poked up and gave a surprised smile. "Oh, hey, guys. How was your dinner?"

"It was great," Derek answered, but then lowered his voice. "Who was that guy you were talking to here at the bar before?"

Nick chuckled. "I talk to a lot of people. That's a big part of the job."

Derek shook his head. "Right, but my brother saw you with a particular guy. He said you looked like you were arguing." Nick looked at Sam questioningly.

Sam sighed and stepped up to the counter. "Tall, thin guy, kinda looked like Abe Lincoln."

"Fisher?" Nick laughed. "I'd never thought of the resemblance before, but now that you mention it, he does sort of look like Honest Abe, but without the honesty part."

"He's dishonest?" asked Caitlin.

Nick groaned. "That's one way to describe it." He eyed them curiously. "What's your interest in Fisher? Do you know him?"

"Not exactly…" Sam's eyes dropped to the wooden counter.

"We call him the Virginia Creeper," said Derek.

Nick was in the middle of a drink of water and nearly choked. He wiped his face and laughed again. "That's even better than Abe Lincoln. Care to explain?"

"Just being funny," Sam answered quickly. "Who is he?"

Nick glanced over at the dining room like he was considering how much to say. He leaned closer across the bar. "Fisher is the outside counsel for Wolf Hills Investments."

"Counsel?" asked Sam.

"It means he's a lawyer." Caitlin stepped closer and met Nick's stare. "He works for Bernard Hostetter?"

"That's right. He's based out of New York most of the time, but he's essentially Bernard's hatchet man."

"Hatchet man?" said Derek.

Nick kept his voice low. "He's been pushing to buy most of the historic buildings around Abingdon."

Caitlin's eyes opened wide. "But why would he want to buy them?"

Nick grabbed a white towel and ran it over the wood. "Nobody really knows for sure, but there've been rumors they're trying to open up some kind of corporate retreat center."

"And he wants to buy The Tavern?" asked Sam.

Nick nodded. "And the Barter, The Martha, and close to a dozen old buildings in the historic district. He'd probably pave a four-lane highway smack over the Creeper Trail if he could."

The door to the street opened and an older couple bustled in. "Is it true that this is the oldest bar in Virginia?" the woman asked.

Nick nodded politely. "Yes, ma'am. That's a fact. Can

I get you something to drink?" He glanced back at them and nodded to the door. "I think you three should get going."

Sam realized how three kids standing at the tiny bar might look out of place, so they waved goodbye and ducked out to the sidewalk. The night breeze was warm, but it felt good on his face. Sam glanced up and down the street and thought about Bernard's investment company trying to buy up the historic district.

Caitlin waved at the brick buildings all around them. "I can't believe someone would want to change all this. Don't people realize how important history is?"

"At least we're getting more clues," said Derek. "Come on, let's get back to The Martha. We can sort things out there."

They strolled silently along the brick sidewalk, each of them lost in thought. So much had happened since they'd arrived in town. It was hard for Sam to even remember his original excitement at getting to watch Jake in the play.

As they approached the corner, his eyes settled on a light on the second floor of one of the old brick buildings. It was *Wolf Hills Investments*. He stopped mid-stride as a tall figure drifted past the window, almost like it was floating.

"What's the matter?" asked Caitlin.

Sam pointed at the window just as the light went out. "Somebody's up there."

Derek followed Sam's stare. "Looks dark to me."

"He was there a minute ago…"

As they watched the window, a heavy wooden door shut ahead of them with a thud. A tall figure stepped out to the sidewalk.

It was Fisher. The Creeper.

The kids ducked behind the nearest tree and watched Fisher lock the building door. He paused and looked both ways cautiously, like a snake testing the air with its tongue. It was almost like Fisher could sense their presence, even though they were well hidden behind the tree. All at once, he turned and decisively strode across the street, making a right on the far sidewalk back toward The Tavern.

When Fisher was well past their hiding spot, Derek stepped out from behind the tree. "Come on, we have to follow him."

Fisher was walking fast, and Derek and Caitlin had already started down the sidewalk in pursuit before Sam could object. He jogged to catch up. "But we're supposed to go straight back to the inn."

"Fine," Derek answered. "You go to the inn, Wienerschnitzel. We're following him."

Sam glared at him. "Don't call me that."

"You said he looked suspicious, remember?" said Caitlin.

Sam's anger at his brother was quickly replaced by thoughts about the Creeper. "Yeah, suspicious like he might be a killer. All the more reason to stay back."

"You're all bark and no bite, Sam," Derek cried. "All smoke and no fire. All wiener and no schnitzel—"

"We get the point, Derek," snapped Caitlin.

Sam felt his anger build again as he picked up his pace. "Fine. We'll follow him. But I don't like it."

They followed Fisher at a distance, keeping at least a block of separation between them. With each passing streetlamp, the kids' shadows leaped ahead of them, growing longer and longer along the sidewalk. The Barter and The Martha were in the other direction. Sam didn't know what was on this side of town, but they continued on briskly for several more blocks.

"What happened to his BMW?" asked Sam. "How come he's walking?"

"Maybe he lives up here," suggested Caitlin, "and just wanted to enjoy the fresh air."

"Maybe he's an ax murderer luring us into a deserted parking lot. You heard what Nick called him, he's a hatchet man."

Caitlin shook her head. "I don't think he meant a literal hatchet, Sam. He meant he carries out Bernard's dirty work."

"Yeah, like late-night murders."

Derek shook his head. "Why do you always have to assume the worst possible scenario? Just once, I'd like to see you throw caution to the wind and see what happens."

Sam felt his neck growing hot. In his mind, chasing around after his brother's half-brained schemes all the time was a pretty risky endeavor. "How about I throw you off a bridge and see what happens then? Why do you have to be such a—"

Caitlin held up her hand and stopped short. "Where'd he go?"

Sam squinted through the dim streetlights. The sidewalk up ahead was empty. He'd only taken his eyes off Fisher for a few moments to think about all reasons his brother was a numbskull. And already his worries were coming true.

"He was right there a second ago." Derek broke into a jog. "He must have turned up one of these side streets. We can't lose him now." He stopped at the next corner and peered through the shadows.

"See anything?" asked Sam as he and Caitlin caught up.

Derek pointed into the distance. "There he is. Moving down the hill past that parking lot. Come on."

Sam had a sinking feeling as they walked down the side road. Main Street had been dark, but the lampposts had helped them see where they were going. This street didn't have any lights, so the sidewalk was steeped in shadows and they'd have to rely on the moonlight. As far as Caitlin's parents knew, they'd gone back to the hotel. If anything happened to them out here, no one would even know where to look.

"You sure he went in there?" asked Caitlin, stopping at the spot they'd seen Fisher turn.

Tall trees loomed in silhouette on all sides of a trail

that darted straight into the woods. "Where are we?" It looked like an entrance to a park. Sam noticed a black iron fence, and for a moment, he thought it was a cemetery. They'd seen a few graveyards around town. That would be a deal breaker.

Caitlin pointed to a huge, dark mass in the shadows behind the fence. As they stepped closer, Sam realized it was a train. They stared up at the black steam engine parked on display under a metal canopy. It looked like someone had taken a locomotive from a giant model train set and placed it by the edge of the trees. Sam read the sign in front. "Old Molly Steam Engine - Norfolk & Western Steam Engine 433."

"It must be one of the Creeper engines," said Derek. "You know, the ones that pulled the trains up through the mountains."

"Now I know where we are." Caitlin walked a few more yards up the path and pointed to a metal bridge that spanned a small creek. "This is the trailhead for the Creeper Trail."

"That's an appropriate place for Fisher to go," said Derek. "The Creeper on the Creeper Trail."

Sam peered up the dark trail. "I'm not going in there. It probably closes after dark anyway."

"Then someone forgot to tell Fisher that," said Caitlin.

"We can't just let him get away. We'll lose his—" Derek stopped mid-sentence as a long, desperate howl pierced the darkness. They eyed each other nervously.

"What was that?" asked Caitlin.

"Probably just a dog," said Derek.

"It didn't sound like any dog I've ever heard." Sam felt his heart beat faster. He stared across the dark landscape. A long slope began to rise on one side of the trail. "Don't you get it? This is Wolf Hills."

"Wolf Hills?" said Derek. "You mean like the investment company?"

"No, weren't you listening to what Ginny said before the play? Wolves attacked Daniel Boone and his dogs, right in this town. Maybe right in this very spot!"

Derek shook his head. "That was ages ago. Remember what Giff and Hudson said? There aren't any wolves here these days."

"Yeah, well, I won't be here either." Sam glanced back toward Main Street. "I'm leaving."

Caitlin shifted her feet on the gravel uneasily. "I think I agree with Sam on this one."

Derek sighed loudly. "Whatever. I'm sure the Creeper is long gone by now, anyway. I might as well be pushing a baby carriage with you two along."

"Hey," huffed Caitlin. "Be nice."

Derek held up his hand and stood frozen. "Shh."

"I'm serious, Derek. I'm leaving." Sam turned around but stopped in his tracks when a branch snapped from behind the locomotive.

"What was that?" Caitlin whispered.

Sam worked to control his breathing, the eerie howl still echoing in his mind. Wolves might not be in

Virginia, but what about coyotes? The creatures could be stalking them, waiting to attack at any moment, just like what had happened to Daniel Boone's hunting party.

"Probably just a squirrel," Derek whispered, but he didn't sound very convinced either. None of them moved as they stared into the blackness and listened.

Another sound came from the woods. This one was closer than the first.

"That was no squirrel," said Sam. It sounded big. Like a wolf.

"I think it's time to go," whispered Caitlin, reaching for Sam's hand.

They took one cautious step forward but then froze again as a shadow emerged from behind the locomotive. It was much too large for a wolf. Was it a bear? No, it was too thin for a bear.

"Good evening," said a deep, silky voice. They knew that voice.

It was Fisher.

The Creeper.

CHAPTER EIGHTEEN

Fisher stepped out from the shadows. He moved close enough that they could see the details of his face, even in the moonlight. It was the first time Sam had been that close to the man.

Fisher was younger than he'd thought. Maybe in his thirties. And despite his tall, thin build, he had the strong, muscular shape of an athlete.

"What do you want?" asked Derek.

Fisher sneered back at them. "I could ask the same question to you, since it appears that you are following me. Or is it just a coincidence that we're all out here on the trail after dark? Perhaps you're simply admiring this old steam engine." He glanced back at the hulking metal train like he held an affection for it.

"Did you know that back in their time, these steam engines required constant fires burning to keep the boiler operating? Firemen fed in shovels of coal, often standing so close that the flames licked their faces at over four hundred degrees. But at least they were mostly safe. The poor lads who laid the tracks over these mountains lost limbs or died in explosions, landslides—it was a dangerous business. All for the sake of progress and to bring expansion westward along the trails that the pioneers had scouted for them."

He paused dramatically, like he could see the locomotive chugging slowly around the mountain turns. "Or perhaps you aren't interested in history."

"We love history," Caitlin said quietly. "But what do you want?"

Fisher grunted. "I want to know why three kids from out of town are suddenly up in my business. Particularly you." He stared at Caitlin. "You're related to Virginia Moss, aren't you?"

"That's right. She's my aunt."

"An interesting woman, that one."

Caitlin stood her ground. "What does she have to do with you?"

Fisher stroked his thin beard. "Let's just say we have a business relationship. And I'll give you a word of advice. You don't want to get in the way of my business. You've no idea who you're dealing with."

A moth fluttered past Sam's ear. It circled them until Fisher suddenly snatched it from the air. "I will crush you." He crumpled the moth in his hand and tossed it to the ground. "Like a bug." His eyes narrowed. "Do we understand each other?"

Sam tried to answer, but his throat felt constricted. It was hard to take a breath. He simply nodded.

"We hear you," Derek replied.

Fisher sighed. "I know you hear me. I need to know that you understand. Those are two different things entirely."

"Yes," said Caitlin. "We understand."

Fisher grinned, and it caught Sam off guard. He had imagined a mouth full of crooked, yellowed teeth, but Fisher's smile was the opposite. Even in the near darkness, Fisher's mouth was filled with two rows of gleaming perfection. Almost like a set of shark teeth.

"Excellent." Fisher took a step backward, the shadows nearly enveloping him. "Then I don't expect that we'll be seeing each other again."

And just like that, he vanished.

Sam blinked and tried to catch his breath. He leaned forward and stared into the darkness, half expecting Fisher to appear again from the shadows, but the trail was empty. He was gone. "Did that just happen?"

Derek shook his head. "What a weirdo. More like Count Dracula than Abe Lincoln, if you ask me."

"I think we need to stop following him." Sam turned and bumped into Caitlin. "Right?" When she didn't answer, he touched her shoulder softly. "Are you okay?"

Caitlin bit her lip like she was about to cry, which would be fine, given that they had just been threatened by an Abe Lincoln vampire lookalike in the middle of the woods. Heck, Sam felt like he might lose it, too. But it took a lot to scare Caitlin. Sam would never admit it in front of Derek, but she was tougher than he was.

"What's wrong?" he asked again.

Caitlin let out a long breath and shook her head. "I'm worried about Aunt Ginny. Why would she be in business with that… thing? Whatever's going on here, she seems to be in the middle of it. First with Jake, now this. What has she gotten mixed up in?"

Sam wanted to say that he knew what she meant, that he was worried about her aunt too, and that if he had to guess, she was up to no good with those envelopes of money. Or even worse, that maybe she'd tried to hurt Jake in the theater. But he couldn't tell her that right now. It would be too cruel.

Instead, he put his arm around her shoulder gently. "I'm sure it will be all right. We'll figure this out."

Caitlin sniffed and took a deep breath. "Thanks." She looked up and glanced around. "Hey, where's Derek?"

Sam had been so focused on Caitlin that he hadn't noticed what his brother was doing. He turned in a circle, scanning the trail. This was the last thing they needed. He spotted a shadow on the other side of the locomotive. Was it his brother, or was Fisher coming back to scare them some more?

"Derek?" Sam felt his insides tighten as the shadow rushed toward them, crunching on the trail's gravel. It skidded to a stop just ahead of them.

It was Derek. On a bike.

"What are you doing?" hissed Sam.

"I found a bike." Derek grinned proudly.

"You found it?" asked Caitlin.

Sam closed his eyes. "You mean you stole it."

"Found, stole—who's to say what the difference is?"

"The police, probably," Sam mumbled.

"I borrowed it. And there's two more, right over there." Derek pointed to a small building on the other side of the trail.

"Why do we need bikes?" asked Caitlin.

"It's a little late to go for another ride on the Creeper Trail, don't you think?" said Sam.

Derek cocked his head. "I decided we need a plan."

"Oh no," said Sam. Things were bad enough without one of Derek's convoluted plans. Why couldn't they just head back to The Martha? "I think we've had enough excitement for one day."

Caitlin put her hand on Sam's arm. "Let's hear him out. What's your plan?"

"Well," Derek started, gesturing with his hands like a conductor. "We have all these confusing clues, but we haven't gone to the source. I want to hear it from the horse's mouth."

"You're going to steal a horse, too?" Sam asked.

Caitlin lowered her eyebrows. "You mean Aunt Ginny?"

"Close, but no." Derek brought his hands together.

"Think the other direction. We need to talk to Greensboro."

"Jake?" That caught Sam by surprise.

Derek nodded. "Jake."

"But isn't he in the hospital?" asked Caitlin.

Derek patted the handlebars on the bike. "That's why we need these."

Sam couldn't hold it in. "We're going to ride to the hospital in the dark? Do you even know where the hospital is? This isn't Richmond, you know. It could be twenty miles from here. It could be back on the interstate highway and over the mountain. We could ride all night. We could—"

"Sam!" Derek shouted. "Chill out, will you?" He held up his phone and flashed a map. "I already looked. It's just a couple miles up the road. Right next to Wal-Mart. Piece of cake."

"Piece of cake..." Sam muttered, trying to think through all the things that could go wrong with his brother's plan.

"What would we do when we got there?" Caitlin asked.

"Go visit Jake's room," Derek replied. "They have visitors at hospitals, right? It's not like he's in intensive care. We met him before the play, so we're not complete strangers. I mean, he's practically your uncle, right?"

Caitlin frowned. "No, he's not. They never got married, and any chance of that was nearly twenty years ago."

Derek shrugged. "Yeah, well, besides that. He could have been."

Sam groaned. "You're crazy."

Derek reached out and poked Sam's forehead playfully. "And you're a Wienerschnitzel. But we have to do something. Come on, get the bikes."

CHAPTER NINETEEN

The ride to the hospital wasn't very far, but Sam couldn't shake the feeling that they should have been pedaling in the opposite direction. He held his breath at each passing car, hoping it wasn't the police. While it was probably too soon for the bikes to have been reported stolen, it had to be against some law to ride after dark without lights and helmets. Whenever they finished whatever this was they were doing, he vowed to return the bikes where they'd found them.

There wasn't much traffic, but they rode on the sidewalks until they ended up near the outskirts of town. Sam spotted the Wal-Mart sign up ahead, glowing like a blue and yellow beacon. Soon they were riding through the sprawling parking lots of the hospital complex. There were more cars than he'd expected for that time of night, but he figured hospitals worked 24/7. They cruised past the ER toward an area marked "lobby" and stowed the bikes in a convenient rack next to the sidewalk.

"Leave the talking to me," Derek said, as they passed through the automatic glass doors. A security guard stood at the side of the room, and Sam hoped they didn't look as guilty as he felt.

Derek marched up to the information desk and smiled at a woman with dark, curly hair. Sam had watched his brother sweet-talk people like this plenty of times, but it still made him nauseous. The security guard didn't seem to be paying them any attention, so Sam tried to relax.

"Hi, there…" Derek leaned closer to read the tag on woman's blouse. "Cassandra. Great name."

She looked up and beamed. "Why, thank you, young man. How can I help you?"

"We're here to visit someone."

Cassandra tapped on her computer keyboard. "Okay. What's the last name?"

"Greensboro."

Sam closed his eyes. He hadn't considered how that would sound. They weren't just asking to visit some random person. Jacob Greensboro was famous. Cassandra had to know that. There was no way that she, or anyone else, was going to let them in. This was a gigantic waste of time.

Cassandra lowered her glasses and stared up at them from her chair. "Are you family of Mr. Greensboro?"

"Well, uh…" Derek answered, "not exactly."

Sam glanced again at the security guard. He'd lowered his newspaper and was now looking in their direction. If Derek started making up stories about lost parakeets again, they'd be done for.

"He's our client," Caitlin replied suddenly.

Sam's head jerked around. He hadn't expected that one.

Apparently, neither had Cassandra. "Excuse me?"

Caitlin nodded confidently. "That's right. My aunt, Virginia Moss, asked us to come speak with him. You might know her. She's the manager over at the Barter Theatre."

"Oh sure, I know Ginny. Well, not closely, mind you, but we used to be in a book club together."

Caitlin laughed. "That sounds like Aunt Ginny, all right. She's a real bookworm. Well, she's tied up tonight, so she asked us to swing by and review some documents with Mr. Greensboro."

Cassandra leaned forward and eyed Caitlin and the boys. "I think we have a problem."

"What's that?"

"I don't see any documents."

Caitlin held up her phone. "They're electronic, of course."

Cassandra let out a cackle. "Oh, well, of course. Everything seems to be that way these days, doesn't it?" Sam couldn't believe it, but the woman seemed like she was actually considering letting them through. "It's awfully late though. Visiting hours are nearly over."

"We'll be quick," Caitlin assured her. "We'd have waited until morning, but it's time sensitive."

"Did you see his last big movie?" Derek interrupted. "*Downtown Panic?*"

Cassandra's eyes widened. "I loved that one. It was so exciting. Is it about that?"

Derek shook his head. "No."

Her expression dropped. "Oh, well, something to do with an upcoming project then?"

"Something like that." Derek lowered his voice. "But we can't talk about it. Highly confidential. I could tell you, but then I'd have to kill you."

"What?" Cassandra raised her eyebrows. Sam glanced back at the security guard, but he'd gone back to his newspaper.

"I'm just kidding. A little show business humor," said Derek.

Cassandra squealed in delight. "Of course. How exciting."

Caitlin cleared her throat and shot Derek a look. "Okay, well, we should get to it. What room is he in?"

Cassandra straightened in her chair and typed into her keyboard. "Oh, yes. Let's see here. I know they placed him over in the new wing for privacy. Hardly anyone over there yet. South wing, Room 307."

Caitlin smiled. "Thank you so much."

* * *

THE ELEVATOR DOORS opened on Floor 3 and Caitlin walked over to a laminated map on the wall. She studied the layout and then pointed to the right. "I think it's down here."

Derek whistled. "This place is bigger than I thought."

"You almost got us busted," Sam scolded.

"Nah. You just have to sell it to make them think it's real."

Sam shook his head. "You're real, all right. Real crazy."

Derek gave him a light shove into the wall. "Hey, we're in, aren't we?"

They followed Caitlin through the winding hallways of the hospital. Cassandra had said Jake's room was in a new wing, and she wasn't kidding. There didn't seem to be anyone around at all. Several of the rooms they passed had furniture stacked in plastic. Some sections still had "Wet Paint" signs on the walls, and large bins of construction materials lined the halls. The longer they walked, the more secluded it became. When they turned down the last hallway, the hospital seemed almost abandoned.

"You sure this is the right place?" asked Sam.

Caitlin pointed at the room numbers next to the doors. "It should be just up here. They said they were giving him privacy."

Sam raised his eyebrows. "This is private, all right. But so is Antarctica."

Around the corner, they found Room 307 on the left.

The door was half-open, and a blue-colored light was flickering from within the darkened room. Sam realized whoever was in there must be watching television. "What if it's not him?"

"Well, then we'll leave," said Caitlin.

Sam glanced around the hall. It felt more like the morgue than a place where any living patients should be kept. "Shouldn't there be nurses, or doctors, or somebody around to take care of him?"

"Maybe they already went home," said Derek.

"No, he's right," replied Caitlin. "There's always a night shift. My grandma was in the hospital last year, and no matter what time it was, there was someone nearby to monitor the patients."

Derek shrugged. "Maybe they're on break." He pointed at the room. "Come on. We don't have a lot of time. Cassandra said visiting hours are almost over."

They stepped to the doorway, and Derek knocked. "Hello, Mr. Greensboro?"

"Come in."

Sam had a strange sense of déjà vu as they rounded the corner into a spacious room. It felt like visiting Jake's dressing room before the play. He knew the actor wouldn't still be in his wolf costume, but he braced himself for a surprise just in case.

There were two beds, but only one of them was occupied. Jake lay on his back with his leg in a cast and elevated. "I hope you brought some actual food this time." He was staring at a car chase scene on the TV and hadn't seen them yet. "I swore to the last nurse that I will not eat any more of that Jell-O, if you could even call it that…"

Caitlin cleared her throat. "Um, Mr. Greensboro?"

He looked up at them in surprise. "Oh. Hello. You're not the nurse."

Caitlin shook her head. "No, I'm Ginny Moss's niece. We met in your dressing room before the show and the…"

"Accident," Derek finished.

Jake coughed. "That was no accident." He leaned forward and glanced toward the hall. "How'd you kids get past the security guard?"

"Security guard?" asked Sam. "You mean the one at the hospital entrance?"

Jake shook his head. "No, right outside in the hallway. They posted one after the second note arrived."

"Second note?" asked Caitlin.

Jake's lips narrowed. "I wouldn't usually say anything about it to you kids, but since you already saw the first one…" He motioned to the chair against the wall.

Caitlin unfolded a piece of paper that had been dropped onto the seat. "You were warned. Now there's only one more trade to make. And this time you won't be so lucky."

"You're sure the guard isn't in the hallway?" Jake asked again.

Sam shook his head. "There's nobody out there. The entire wing is like a ghost town."

Jake switched off the television with a remote. His face turned serious. "Okay, I need you three to listen carefully and do exactly what I say, understand?"

They all nodded in surprise.

Jake reached for his phone and grabbed a couple items from the bedside table. He patted the side of the bed rail. "These things are all on wheels. You need to release the brakes along the bottom, and then you're going to wheel me out of here."

"The whole bed?" asked Derek.

Jake glanced at his leg. "Don't think I'll be making a run for it without a set of wheels."

"But who are we running from?" Sam asked.

"Shouldn't you stay where you are, given your condition?" said Caitlin.

Jake gathered his sheets into the middle of the bed. "I'll be fine, but something's not right. Maybe I've played too many detective roles over the years, but I have a sixth sense about things being off. And something is definitely wrong here." He nodded to the bed wheels. "Come on now. Let's get this thing moving."

Sam and Caitlin reached under each of the four corners and turned the wheel locks. Then Derek moved behind the hospital bed and gently pushed it like a shopping cart. He carefully navigated around the corner and through the threshold of the doorway. "Where are we headed?"

Jake pointed at a dark room across the hall two doors up. "Let's try that one."

The bed glided easily along the tile floor. When they reached the new room, they carefully slid into an open space along the back wall.

"Are you still okay?" Caitlin asked.

"I'll live," said Jake. "Thanks for the help."

Derek glanced around the dark room. "What do we do now?"

"We wait and see what happens."

"That's it?"

"Sometimes that's all you can do." Jake turned and eyed them carefully. "You three never said what you were doing here, by the way. It's a little late for a casual hello."

"We needed to talk to you," said Caitlin.

Jake stared at their serious faces. "Why do I get the feeling you don't have standard fan questions?"

"It's about my aunt Ginny."

"What about her?"

Caitlin fidgeted with her hair. "About you and her."

Jake sat quietly for a moment and then nodded. "I was wondering how many people she'd told about those days."

"She didn't tell anyone, or at least not us," said Caitlin.

"We figured it out from one of the cast pictures in the hallway at the Barter," explained Derek. "The two of you looked pretty friendly with each other."

Jake chuckled. "Yes, you could say that. What can I tell you? We were in love."

Caitlin's face turned red, like she was about to burst.

"Then why did you break her heart?" she practically shouted. She seemed to realize that she was yelling and closed her eyes. "I'm sorry. It's just that I'm worried about her."

"Worried about her?" asked Jake. "Why?"

"We'll tell you in a minute," Caitlin answered. "But first, I want you to tell us what happened back then."

Jake stared at the empty wall across from the bed like he was watching a scene play out in his memory. He slowly shook his head. "I've always regretted how things ended with Ginny. She deserved better. Much better. But my life seemed like it was a rocket ship back then, and I let some people get burned."

He told them he'd had no intention of leaving her, but when his first big film, *Panama Conspiracy*, blew up out of the gate, it suddenly thrust him into the world of celebrity.

"I wasn't ready for it. I can see that clearly now. But back then, I was young and cocky. I didn't know how to handle the success and it went to my head.

"It took me far too long to realize, but I owe a lot to the Barter. This little town was where everything started for me, and Abingdon will always hold a special place in my heart. As will Ginny. When I learned the theater was struggling, I thought performing here could help give it a nice boost.

"I didn't know Ginny was still working here, but I was happy when I heard, and glad she was doing well. I tried to meet with her privately so we could talk through what had happened in our past, but she wasn't interested. She said all that was water under the bridge. She said that she'd moved on and was just thankful for the added attention I might bring to the theater."

"I'll bet you didn't expect to end up in here." Derek glanced around the hospital room.

"I certainly didn't. But I've had a lot of time to reflect, lying in this bed the past couple of days. And the truth is, my motives for coming back weren't quite as pure as I've let on."

Sam's eyebrows raised. "They weren't?"

"It's difficult for me to admit." Jake looked away, his shoulders slumped. "But my career isn't in good shape."

"What are you talking about?" asked Derek. "You're famous!"

"Sure. But fame is fleeting. The ride down can be just as swift as the ascent to the top. Often it is much faster."

"That's impossible," said Sam. "The Clint Patterson movies are my favorites."

"Mine too, Sam, but it's been nearly five years since I last filmed one of those movies. As popular as they once were, that's also the only way the movie industry sees me —as a daring detective. Have you noticed any of my recent work? Guest-hosting reality TV shows and pitching comfortable sneakers? That's the actor I've become."

Sam thought about it and realized maybe it had been a while since the last Clint Patterson movie.

"But the Barter was special," Jake continued. "I saw

an opportunity to rekindle some of that magic from the early days. When my agent got the call that they were looking for someone who had worked here before to come back for a special performance, I knew it was the right thing to do. I've always loved the stage. I decided I needed to get back to my roots and perform in front of an audience, back where it all began. And now this…"

A door closed somewhere far down the hallway and everyone tensed. Jake seemed genuinely worried, but he *was* an actor, after all. How were you supposed to know when he was telling the truth or just putting you on? Faking or not, someone was definitely coming. They listened silently as footsteps echoed through the vacant halls.

Derek motioned for Sam and Caitlin to crouch behind the bed. Sam huddled next to Caitlin and watched the hallway through an opening in the metal frame. The steps stopped right outside Jake's original room. Who could be wandering around the deserted hall? Was it a nurse or a doctor checking up on Jake? Or maybe it was really just the missing security guard coming back to his post. Or was it the author of the letters, the death threats, coming to finish the job they'd started back at the Barter?

Sam held his breath in anticipation. Was this the part of the movie when the gangsters pulled out their guns and sprayed the bed with bullets? The footsteps moved again along the tile floor. Whoever was out in the hall was coming toward their room.

A chill ran down Sam's spine. How did they always end up in these situations? He inched further into the shadows to stay out of sight from the doorway. As he slid backward, his hip bumped into a metal cabinet. He peered up as a stainless-steel tray wobbled, and then slipped from the edge of the table.

Time seemed to stand still. If that tray hit the tile floor, it would clang louder than an orchestra cymbal. Sam lunged. His elbow banged on the tile, but his fingers grabbed the metal tray just before it reached the floor.

He exhaled silently and turned back toward the door, clutching the tray in his hand. That was a close one. Caitlin leaned back to see what he was doing. As she did, her arm collided with his, knocking the metal tray from his grasp. It spun across the room and crashed into the wall with a clatter.

The footsteps ran through the doorway.

A hand flicked on the light switch.

CHAPTER TWENTY

I t took a second for their eyes to adjust to the lights, but Caitlin quickly jumped from her hiding spot behind the bed. "Aunt Ginny!"

"Caitlin? What in the world are you doing here?" She stared at Jake in the hospital bed and only seemed more confused. "Is everything all right? Jake, I thought your room was down the hall."

"It was… it is…" For once, the movie star seemed tongue-tied trying to explain what was happening. "I think maybe we all let our imaginations get the best of us."

Sam shook his head. "It wasn't just our imaginations."

"What are you doing here, Ginny?" Derek cried. "Or maybe I should call you *Virginia*! Who even knows what your real name is?"

Sam leaned over and whispered in Derek's ear. "Ginny's a nickname for Virginia, dummy."

Caitlin's aunt looked overwhelmed as she searched for words. "I… I came here to speak with Jake. There are some things I needed to tell him."

"I knew it!" declared Derek. He picked up the death threat that Jake had showed them and held it in the air. "So you wrote the second letter?"

"Derek…" Sam started, but there was no stopping his brother when he got going. Despite their suspicions about the woman, Sam wasn't sure that this was the best way to get to the bottom of things.

Ginny raised her eyebrows. "Letter?"

Derek stepped around the side of the bed and handed her the paper. She read it and looked up in alarm. "Did you tell the police about this?"

Jake nodded. "They sent a security guard… or at least, I thought they had."

Ginny looked like she was going to be ill. "I can't believe this is still happening." She sat wearily in the chair by the window. "I'm getting even more confused than I was before, and given the past few days, that's saying something."

"What Derek's trying to say, Aunt Ginny—" Caitlin began, but she stopped as Jake held up his hand.

"I think I see what they're up to, Ginny. Or at least part of it." Jake propped himself up higher in the bed on a pillow. "The kids came in here asking about you and me from our times together back in the theater company. With what happened last night on the stage, I think finding out we have a history has led them to some extreme conclusions…"

Ginny looked up at them, startled. "Oh, my goodness. You couldn't possibly think that I…" Her voice trailed off without finishing, as if the idea was too terrible to utter aloud.

Derek placed his hands on his hips. "Are you saying you didn't arrange to have Jake knocked out during the show? I suppose you're denying writing the threatening letters, too."

The woman stared at them blankly. "I would never, I mean, I could never hurt anyone—Jake or otherwise." A tear trickled down her cheek as she searched the faces around the room. "How could you think that?" When her eyes reached her niece, the waterworks really started. "Caitlin?"

Caitlin lowered her head. "It was getting hard to know what to believe, Aunt Ginny. I never would have imagined it in a million years, but then we started finding out all these secrets."

"Secrets?"

Caitlin gestured to Jake on the bed. "Why didn't you tell us you two had dated when you were younger?"

Ginny sighed. "It was so long ago, honey. And frankly, I was embarrassed. No one likes to admit to being left on the scrap heap while their boyfriend went on to fame and riches."

That seemed to hit Jake hard. His face crumbled. "Ginny…."

Caitlin's aunt took a tissue from the table and wiped her eyes. She blew her nose and sat straight in her chair. "No, it's okay. I got over you a long time ago, Jake. I moved on, and while I'll admit it was a tad awkward having you back here at the theater, we're different people now. I was happy for the good that could come from your being a part of this production."

Derek scratched his head and glanced at Sam. "But what about the payoff? We saw you pull an envelope of cash from the shelf in the theater."

Ginny's eyes widened. "Envelope from the shelf… how could you know that? No one else was in there this afternoon but me."

"We were in the wardrobe room," explained Caitlin. "We heard you coming down the hall and accidentally hid in the tunnel."

Sam held back a shiver as he recalled that dark place. "You locked us in when you shut the door."

Ginny nearly fell off the chair. "Locked you in the tunnel! I never even saw you—" She seemed to finally remember closing the door on her way out. "Oh, no!"

Even Jake looked surprised at that news. "The Civil War tunnel? That was a dangerous place back in my time. Certainly no place to be hiding. You could have been killed."

"We found our way to the other entrance in The Martha," explained Sam.

"But, Aunt Ginny," Caitlin said hesitantly, "what were you doing?"

"Yeah," said Derek. "What was in the envelope? Why would you be working with Fisher if it didn't have something to do with offing Greensboro?"

Sam glared at him, trying to tell him to take it easy. It was one thing to ask some questions, but this wasn't the police station.

Ginny grew quiet. She stared at her shoes like she was gathering her thoughts. "I had nothing to do with the accident or the threatening letters," she finally said. "But I've got plenty of things I'm not proud of."

Jake stared at her. "What have you done, Ginny?"

She shook her head slowly. "I am working with Fisher, but it's not what you think."

"It never is," muttered Derek.

Ginny leaned against the windowsill and stared at the parking lot lights. She let out a long breath and then turned back to them. "The Barter has been in financial trouble. I told you that. But that wasn't the entire truth. I was out of cash as well. I was a step away from bankruptcy. So I dipped into the theater's central fund to pay a few bills."

Caitlin gasped and closed her eyes.

"It was just a couple times," Ginny cried. "I swore that I'd pay it all back with interest before anyone even noticed. But when the economy tanked, Bernard offered to take on a share of the theater to help maintain its operations. "

"You told us that last part," said Caitlin. "But wouldn't that have been helpful?"

Ginny nodded. "It was, at first. But during their due diligence, Bernard and his goon, Fisher, went through the financial books. Let's face it, I've always been better with the performance side of the theater than the business side. I guess I hadn't hidden my little loans as well I as I thought I had.

"They threatened to expose me. Not only would I face bankruptcy, I'd be facing criminal charges. It would be a scandal, and I couldn't put the theater through that. Whatever mistakes I'd made, it wasn't the Barter's fault, and I couldn't bear to be the one who brought down its reputation after all these years."

"So what happened?" asked Sam.

"Surprisingly, they offered to help me out with a loan so I could pay back the theater. That's what those cash payments are for. Except there were strings attached. They said they'd turn me in if I didn't agree to cut them an even bigger ownership share of the theater. I've tried to tell them I can't make those decisions without the board, but they won't listen. Soon after, I started hearing rumblings around town that WHI was buying up properties to turn Abingdon's historic district into a modern convention center and an amusement park. I was horrified, but they had me. I was trapped, and there was nothing I could do about it."

"That's extortion, Ginny," said Jake.

She shrugged. "I was in too deep. It was hard to think clearly."

Sam didn't know what to think of that story, but

Caitlin walked over and buried her face in her aunt's arms. "I'm so sorry. That's just terrible."

"I'm the one who should be sorry, dear. I've made such a mess of things." She raised her head and looked Caitlin in the eye. "But I promise you, I had nothing to do with the letters or the accident at the show." She shook her head slowly. "That's what makes all this that much more troubling."

Jake shifted his weight in the bed and groaned at the pain in his leg. "I wish you'd reached out to me, Ginny. I could have helped you."

"I'm sorry for the secrets. Once you start down a dark hole like that, it's hard to get back to the light."

Derek tilted his head. "So, if you didn't send the letters or cause the accident at the Barter, who did?"

"I've been lying here wracking my brain," said Jake, "but I can't come up with anything."

"It has to be Bernard and Fisher," said Sam. "Doesn't it?" He told them about how Fisher had confronted them by the locomotive.

Ginny sat back in the chair next to the bed. "But what does Jake have to do with my problems? Or even with WHI's attempts to take over the town?"

"Maybe they're intending on shutting down the theater for all their big plans," said Caitlin. "And disrupting the production would be an easy way to close things down. Could they buy it for a lower price if the show fails?"

Sam considered what Caitlin had said, but everything

seemed confusing now. He yawned as a wave of tiredness swept over him.

Ginny seemed to notice and looked at her watch. "It's late, kids. Caitlin, do your parents know where you all are?" From the look on Caitlin's face, it was clear that she hadn't checked in with them. Ginny nodded and pulled out her phone. "Okay. Well, let me do that now. They're probably wondering where you three are." She typed in a quick text. "There, that should help—"

She stopped mid-sentence, trying to act like she was fine, but it wasn't a very good act.

"What's wrong?" asked Sam.

"I know a bad cover when I see one," said Jake. "What happened?"

Caitlin put her hand on her aunt's shoulder. "No more lies."

Ginny closed her eyes. "I just received a message from Fisher. He wants to meet me at the theater. Tonight."

CHAPTER TWENTY-ONE

Ginny wanted to bring the kids back to The Martha, but Jake insisted they all come along to the Barter. He wanted to make sure Ginny was safe. Sam really didn't know if that was a good idea with his broken leg, but Jake said he'd practically abandoned Ginny years ago, and he would not leave her to fight off the creepy lawyer by herself now.

Sam didn't know exactly what they could do about it if Fisher really was behind all of this. If he'd already tried to take out a famous actor, he might be more than happy to do away with the rest of them too. Caitlin argued that if Fisher really wanted to hurt them, he'd had ample opportunity when they were alone with him on the Creeper Trail in the dark.

They found a wheelchair in one of the empty rooms and snuck out a back exit of the hospital. Apparently, patients couldn't just walk out of the hospital whenever they wanted, but Jake said this was a special circumstance and he'd come back when they were done. It wasn't easy getting Jake in and out of Ginny's car, but once he was in, at least the wheelchair folded and they could stow it in the back.

"What does Fisher want, anyway?" asked Derek as they drove along Main Street.

That was something Sam had wondered about too. Maybe he was going to talk to her about seeing the kids on the trail or demand that she close the theater for good.

"There's no telling with him," Ginny replied. "But as I told you before, I've put myself in such a tight situation, there's been little I could say about anything he asked of me."

Jake put his hand on her shoulder. "Let me do the talking. You said they're businessmen. When money talks, they'll listen."

Sam wondered if Jake had watched too many of his own movies. But limping in and out of the wheelchair with his leg in a cast certainly didn't portray the same image as he had in his action flicks. Real life was a little different from up on the big screen. Riding in the car together, Jake just seemed like a normal guy.

They parked right out front of the Barter in a no-parking, handicapped zone. Ginny didn't seem to be too concerned. And Derek pointed out that they had someone in a wheelchair, but Sam was pretty sure you needed a special tag for that. Maybe in a small town like

Abingdon, they weren't as strict about things like parking late at night.

Ginny unlocked the entrance, and Derek wheeled Jake up the ramp and through the front doors. The lobby was dark, but they continued through the main doors to the auditorium. The ghost light was dim up on the stage, but Sam noticed a tall, thin shadow beside one of the curtains. Fisher.

Ginny moved to the wall and turned on some additional lights. She took the handles of the wheelchair from Derek and motioned to the back row. "You kids stay back here, okay?"

Derek frowned. "But what if you need us?"

"I think we can handle it," said Jake. "We'll give you a signal if it's time to call for backup." He made his best tough-guy face. "It gets pretty hot down in Panama."

Sam tried to laugh, but his nerves got the best of him. It wasn't every day that your favorite movie star said his signature line to your face. But honestly, that was the last thing on his mind right now. He glanced up at Fisher and gulped. "I guess…"

Ginny wheeled Jake up the right side aisle. Fisher stepped down from the stage and stood with them near the first row. He stared across the theater and glared at the three kids in the back.

"What's *he* doing here?" they heard Fisher ask Ginny about Jake. Even in the back row, the theater's acoustics allowed them to hear pretty well.

"I came to look you in the eye," Jake answered.

The tall man looked down at Jake, who was confined to the chair. "You're a little low for that, I'm afraid."

"Why are you sending me those letters?" Jake replied.

"I hate to burst your ego, Mr. Greensboro, but I'm not much of a film buff. You didn't receive fan mail from me."

Jake's hands were poised on the wheelchair handles like he was about to jump up and strike, even though that was close to impossible with his bum leg. "And the accident up there on the stage? You had nothing to do with that?"

Fisher looked insulted. "Mr. Greensboro, I'm a lawyer, not a hit man. This isn't one of your action scenes. And I resent the implication. My arrangement with Ms. Moss is an investment opportunity. Plain and simple."

Derek leaned across the row and whispered to Sam and Caitlin. "Do you believe him?"

Sam shrugged. "I don't know what to believe anymore."

If it hadn't been for Jake in the wheelchair, Sam almost felt like he could have been at the movies. The line between fiction and reality had grown thin.

"I feel like we're missing something," Caitlin whispered as her phone buzzed. "It's my mom. She wants us to come back to The Martha."

"What about all this?" asked Derek. "It's about to get good."

Caitlin shook her head. "There's not much more we can do, and I don't want her to get any madder than she probably already is. I don't think anyone is in danger down there. I trust Aunt Ginny to tell us what happened tomorrow."

Derek looked disappointed. "I guess."

Caitlin slipped down the aisle and whispered to her aunt that they were leaving. Ginny turned and waved goodbye. She flashed a smile, but Sam thought it looked forced. He didn't know what they were going to be able to work out, but for the moment, it didn't appear Fisher had planned anything violent.

"Hold on, I need to use the restroom," said Caitlin as they entered the lobby.

Sam yawned again and realized how tired he was. He stared across the theater lobby and past the box office. It seemed so different without crowds of people filing through for a show. He glanced back toward the auditorium and, for the first time, noticed a large painting of a gray-haired Robert Porterfield smiling back at him.

Sam had forgotten all about what he'd seen up in the balcony at the show. Had that really happened? Every-thing was cloudy now. Maybe this place just cast a spell over people when they entered. It was like it was part of the experience of suspending reality to become fully absorbed into the performance.

"Guys, come here!" Caitlin called from around the corner.

Sam walked back to the other side of the lobby. Caitlin stood by a wall lined with photographs. Just like the one downstairs, this wall was filled with pictures of famous performers who'd graced the Barter stage.

"What is it?" Sam looked up at where she was staring. It was an arranged photo of a full cast from an old production. Jacob Greensboro was in the center, smiling widely. Sam turned to Caitlin. "Another picture of Jake. So?"

"Look who's behind him."

Sam pushed up his glasses higher on his nose and leaned closer to the frame. A man was seated in the next row. He was staring at Jake, his expression stuck in a dark glare.

Derek stepped behind them and whistled. "If looks could kill. Who is that guy?"

Sam caught his breath as he stared at the face glaring at Jake twenty years ago. "Oh, my gosh."

It was Nick.

CHAPTER TWENTY-TWO

"Are you sure it's Nick?" asked Derek as they huddled around the photo on the wall.

"Sure looks like it," said Caitlin. "Remember when we met him in the library? He said that he worked at the theater years ago and at the same time as Aunt Ginny. But I never considered that he might have worked alongside Jake."

"What do we even know about him?" asked Derek.

"We know he tried to run a few businesses, but now he's a bartender at The Tavern," said Sam.

"Alexi said he has two kids," added Caitlin, "and it sounded like he might be having a tough time with his marriage. Didn't Alexi say he slept in a room above The Tavern sometimes?"

Sam scanned the list of names at the bottom of the picture. Sure enough, listed as one of the leads was

Nicholas Bulgari. It surprised him that Jacob Greensboro's name wasn't in that section.

As Sam kept reading, he found Jake's name way down near the bottom of the list. Sam re-read the words to make sure he'd seen them right. "That's weird. It says that Jake was an understudy."

"You mean Nick?" asked Caitlin. "You said Jake, but understudy means a backup to the lead performer."

Sam rolled his eyes. "I know what it means, Caitlin. But look right here." He pointed back to the list. "*Nick* was the lead. *Jake* was an understudy."

"How could that be?" asked Derek. "Jake's the one who became a big star."

Sam's eyes moved back to the two men in the picture. The details were grainy, but he squinted and stared closer. Nick was oddly positioned in a chair. Sam pointed at the spot in the photo. "What's he doing with his leg?"

Caitlin studied it and her jaw dropped. "It's a cast. His leg must have been broken."

"No way," muttered Sam.

Derek leaned in over their shoulders. "That's either one heck of a coincidence, or something fishy's going on."

Sam stared at the expression on Nick's face. Derek was right—if looks could kill, then Jake would be dead. He thought about why Jake would stand in the middle if he was supposed to be the understudy. "What if Jake took over the lead after Nick broke his leg?"

"He Wally Pipped him," exclaimed Derek.

Caitlin turned and stared at him. "What?"

"Wally Pipp. Dad told me about him. He was a baseball player for the Yankees. He was a great power hitter, but one day he had a headache and took a game off."

"Nick has a broken leg in the picture," said Sam, "not a headache."

"That's not the point. The person who filled in for Pipp was a young player named Lou Gehrig. That day, he started his consecutive game streak of over 2,000 games in a row. They called him the Iron Horse."

Sam remembered the story now. Gehrig had held the record for most consecutive games played for decades until Cal Ripken broke it in the '90s.

"Oh," said Caitlin. "I see what you mean now." She walked to the lobby door and stared up the street. "So, if Jake filled in for Nick in the lead role, and then Jake became rich and famous, how do you think Nick would feel when he heard Jake was coming back to town?"

"Probably pretty angry," said Sam.

"Like he'd want to get revenge," added Derek.

Caitlin nodded. "I think so too. They have to be connected."

Derek walked up to Caitlin at the window. "Are you thinking what I'm thinking?"

Sam stepped between them and shook his head. He'd seen that look before, and it never led to anything good. "Absolutely not." He pointed into the theater and lowered his voice. "We have enough to worry about with Fisher and whatever problems your aunt has gotten into.

We should go tell them who we think is behind the letters before things get worse."

Derek folded his arms. "How could anything get any worse?"

Sam opened his mouth to object, but Caitlin stopped him. "As much as this all makes sense, we still don't have proof. We can't just march in there and tell Jake that Nick tried to kill him. We need evidence before making an accusation like that."

"We could ask his dad," suggested Sam. "Alexi might help fill in some details."

Caitlin shrugged. "I don't know if he'd want to turn in his son. He probably doesn't even know."

Derek opened the door and stepped out onto the sidewalk. "Well, what are we waiting for? Let's go."

"Go where?" asked Sam.

Derek pointed down the hill toward The Tavern. "I think we need to go pay our old friend Nick a visit."

SAM AND CAITLIN huddled behind a tree outside The Tavern as Derek peeked in the front window. "Do you see him?" Sam whispered.

"I can't see the bar." Derek leaned closer to the glass but shook his head and crept back to the tree. "The lights are on but chairs are on most of the tables like someone's cleaning up."

"How are we supposed to get in there?" asked Sam.

"He'll see us if we walk through the front door." He remembered how the entrance opened straight to the bar and host stand. There was no way they could slip in discretely. They were planning on getting up into the apartment above the Tavern and finding some kind of connection to the accident or the letters that they could pin on Nick. Relying on a dirty look in a picture from twenty years ago probably wouldn't be enough when trying to convince people like the police.

Derek pointed down the path along the side of the building. "What about if we go through the back? We could blend in with the crowd on the patio."

"You just said they're cleaning up. There's no crowd this late," said Caitlin.

Derek sighed impatiently. "Well, while you two sit here and think of a better plan, I'll be inside finding clues."

"You think they'll just be lying around?" asked Sam.

"Maybe."

"Hold on." Caitlin held up her phone. "I have a better idea. We need a distraction. Go read me the phone number off that menu in the front window."

Derek read off the number, and Caitlin quickly explained her plan. They moved to a better hiding spot across the street and under a deep shadow as she dialed the number.

"The Tavern," a woman's voice said over the speaker. Sam thought it might be Tessa.

Caitlin nodded for Derek to talk. "Yes, hello," he

grumbled in the deepest voice he could muster. He was trying not to sound like a kid, but it sounded ridiculous. "I need to speak to Nick, the bartender, please."

"One moment."

There was a pause and they waited silently in the glow of the phone screen, until finally, they heard the clang of glasses in the background.

"This is Nick."

"I know about the letters," said Derek.

"Who is this?"

"The accident at the theater. I know it was you, Nick."

The line was silent for a moment. "What do you want?"

Sam gulped, knowing the tough part was coming up.

"We need to meet," Derek answered. "Tonight."

They could almost hear the gears working in Nick's mind as he considered his options. "Where?"

"At the Creeper trailhead, by the old locomotive. Be there in ten minutes. Come alone."

"Ten minutes?" said Nick. "I'm closing up here and—"

Caitlin tapped the End Call button quickly.

"Why didn't you let him answer?" asked Sam.

"What's the point?" She tucked the phone back in her pocket. "I didn't want to give him time to argue. If he's going to come, he'll do it."

They turned and stared across the quiet street to The

Tavern. "Do you think he'll take the bait?" Sam whispered.

Derek nodded. "He'll come. If it was really him that sent the letters, he can't afford to leave any loose ends."

Sam glanced at his watch. He supposed it made sense that the man would need a couple of minutes to tell any other workers he was leaving suddenly. They'd picked the old locomotive because it was close enough that he might agree to meet there, but far enough away to give them time to search the upstairs room.

A panicked thought flashed through Sam's mind. "What if he goes out the back? We won't see him—"

But before he could finish, the front door opened. Nick stepped out to the sidewalk. He paused, glancing around suspiciously. Sam held his breath. Even though they were all the way across the street, he inched deeper into the shadows.

Nick turned and strode down the sidewalk toward the road that led to the Creeper Trail. As soon as he was out of sight, Derek sprang from the darkness and jogged across the street. They'd decided it would be too conspicuous for all three of them to enter the building. That was fine with Sam, so he'd agreed to keep watch with Caitlin outside. Derek padded along the side of the building, slipped through the gate in the fence, and disappeared.

"What if he comes back?" Sam asked nervously.

Caitlin patted his knee. "Even if he runs to the locomotive, it takes at least five minutes each way. Derek will be fine."

Sam looked back at the Tavern. Even though he wasn't the one sneaking inside, his stomach was still in knots. The upstairs window that faced the side alley started to glow with a dull light. Caitlin's phone buzzed, and she clicked on the speaker.

"I'm upstairs," Derek's voice whispered. "In his office."

"We see your light," said Sam. "Try to keep it low. Someone might notice."

"They certainly won't notice you, Sam," his brother replied testily. "Since you were too chicken to come in here."

"Stop," Caitlin scolded. "We don't have time for arguing. Nick will be back soon. Focus on the room. What do you see in there?"

Even through the phone, they could hear the old floorboards creak under Derek's weight as he walked through the room. Sam hoped no one in the restaurant below would notice.

"There's not much up here," answered Derek. "Just a pull-out futon, some boxes, and a pile of clothes. The dude seriously needs to do some laundry."

"What about the letters?" whispered Caitlin. "Do you see anything?"

Sam glanced at his watch. It had been nearly five minutes. They were running out of time. The flashlight flickered around behind the window.

"I'm checking the desk." They heard drawers opening. The connection got fuzzy for a second, but they heard him saying, "Old menus, bills… hang on, here's a folder. Let me see what's in here…"

The line was silent. "Derek?" asked Sam.

"Bingo," he whispered. "Oh, man. You won't believe what's in this folder—"

"What did you find?" asked Caitlin.

Derek's voice came back sounding mechanical and garbled. They couldn't understand anything he'd said. Maybe someone in the kitchen was running an appliance that was interfering with the signal.

"Derek, say again?" Caitlin held the phone closer to her mouth. They strained to listen for his answer when a car screeched to a halt along the curb. Nick jumped out of the driver's seat and ran to the sidewalk. He stood with his hands on his hips, staring around Main Street in the eerie glow of streetlights.

Sam thought his heart might explode. They hadn't considered Nick *driving* to the locomotive. How had they been so stupid? That meant he'd be back in half the time.

"Derek!" Sam leaned close to the phone in a panic. "Get out of there. Nick's back!"

He turned his attention over to the sidewalk, but Nick had vanished.

"He went inside!" cried Caitlin, standing from the shadows. "We have to do something!"

"Derek, can you hear us?" Sam yelled into the phone. It was too late for whispering. He ran with Caitlin out into the street to get a better view of the second-floor window.

They stood on the double yellow line as bright lights filled the upstairs room. Derek was backed up against the windowpane, a desperate expression on his face.

"Oh, he can hear you all right," Nick's voice said over the phone. "And so can I."

Then the line went dead.

CHAPTER TWENTY-THREE

Derek tried to peer down at Sam and Caitlin, but all he saw were reflections against the glass. Had they heard him say what was in the folder before Nick stormed in and grabbed his phone? Were they still out there, or had they run for help?

"What are you doing up here?" Nick growled.

"Hang on. You mean this isn't the way to the kitchen? I was trying to compliment the chef on the Wiener-schnitzel. I must have made a wrong turn."

"Save it." Nick pointed at the folder in Derek's hands. "Get a good look?"

Derek shook his head. "I, uh, didn't open it yet, sorry. What's in there? More menus?"

The truth was, Derek had already seen a lot more than menus inside the wide manilla folder. It held dozens of printouts and clippings from websites and magazines. All about Jacob Greensboro. Either Nick was the president of Jake's fan club or he was a stalker. The kind that might go to great lengths to hurt a famous star he felt had wronged him. It was all the proof they needed to implicate Nick in the accident, or at the very least, make him a significant suspect for questioning. But first, Derek needed to get it, and himself, out of the room.

Nick stepped closer. "Nice try. I was an actor once, remember? I can spot a fake a mile away." He glanced out the window in the Barter's direction. For a moment, it seemed like his mind was back in time. Derek had thought Nick looked youthful, but now the man seemed weary, like he'd aged since they'd seen him at the bar earlier.

"I don't know who you kids think you are, but this is all none of your business. Do you understand me?"

Derek nodded silently. Talking his way out of things was usually his number-one option, but something in Nick's eyes told him it was better to stay quiet.

"Everything seemed so much simpler back then. We were all young and loved performing. Being on that stage in front of an audience was unlike anything I'd ever experienced. It was what I was born to do. Does that make sense?"

Derek nodded again, wondering what the man would say next. He eyed the room discreetly, searching for something to use as a distraction, a weapon, or another exit he hadn't seen before, but it was pretty sparse.

"I was the leading man," Nick moaned wistfully. "Jake was just this other guy who'd wandered into the group. Sure, he was charming and handsome, but no one took him too seriously. He cared more about getting the girls to like him than the audience, until the last show, at least.

"It was all working out. I was going to hit it big. Get out of this sleepy little town and make something of myself. The crowd was eating out of my hand until somehow, I missed my mark in an action sequence. My foot slipped and I tumbled into the Trap Room. Broke my leg in three places." He reached down and patted his knee.

"But even then, I knew I'd be back. The director loved me nearly as much as the audience did. But the next night, things went sideways. They moved Greensboro into my role. He wasn't even my understudy, just another guy in a minor supporting role. But my usual backup was sick, so Jake got his chance."

Derek already knew the ending, but even so, he hung on every word. Nick's voice raged with emotion, rising and falling like ocean swells. Maybe this was how he'd been as an actor up on stage, but Derek couldn't look away as Nick told his story.

"Again, I wasn't concerned. In fact, I was going to enjoy watching the kid make a fool of himself. I'd have the cast removed soon and then the spotlight would be back on me, where it belonged." He paused and stared at Derek incredulously, like he still couldn't believe what happened next himself. "But you know what?"

Derek resisted the urge to make a joke. "He was good."

Nick swatted at the air. "He was more than good. He was unbelievable. I don't know how it happened, but there was something about that role that was perfect for him. He captured lightning in a bottle that night. Jake became that character—he didn't even have to act. And as fate would have it, one of the most influential producers in Hollywood was sitting in the front row.

"And that was it." Nick bit his lip and seemed to stare right through Derek's head. "Jake went on to fame and stardom, and I... well, what can I say? I'm wiping down the bar each night."

"At least it's a famous bar..." Derek joked, but Nick didn't seem to hear him.

"What about my fame and glory?" Nick's face was reddening like everything inside him was about to explode because of twenty years of frustration.

Derek knew he had to get out of there. Nick was spiraling into a dangerous place. He'd already tried to take out Jake. Derek didn't want to be next. Then a plan slowly formed in his mind, the kind of plan that always made Sam nervous. It could be just the thing to get him out of that room, or it could go terribly wrong. But what other choice did he have?

He took a breath and then broke into a laugh, slapping his knee. "You're a real piece of work, man. You had me going there for a minute."

Nick blinked, glaring like he'd almost forgotten Derek was still there. "Excuse me?"

"All that stuff about being a better actor than Jake? I

mean, come on. You're talking about *Jacob Greensboro*, man. Clint Patterson. *Panama Conspiracy*. I think you've been doing some drinking yourself down there at the bar, because you're talking kinda crazy."

Nick's face turned purple. "I'd advise you to shut your mouth, kid, or you'll find out exactly how serious I am."

Derek gave his best smirk. "Oh really? Then why don't you show me? Right now. Tonight." He nodded toward Main Street. "Out there on the Barter stage where you were supposedly so great." He paused for effect. "At least, when you weren't falling down like a klutz."

He held his wide grin for a ten-count, even though inside his heart was beating out of control. He braced himself for impact just in case the angry man tackled him or swung a punch.

It was possible Derek had overplayed his hand. Likely, even. He may have underestimated this guy. Nick was still blocking the doorway. There was no way Derek could make it around him. Were they too high up to jump out the window?

Nick grabbed Derek's arm in a flash. Derek considered himself strong, but Nick was a grown man and outweighed him by at least fifty pounds. He didn't stand a chance in a fight. But instead of throwing Derek against the wall, Nick pushed him toward the doorway.

"You want a show? Fine. We'll go to the theater. You'll have your show. But trust me when I tell you, it might be the last performance you ever see."

CHAPTER TWENTY-FOUR

S am and Caitlin didn't have many options. Or at least not many good ones. They could burst into The Tavern to help Derek, but maybe that would just get them all captured. It seemed like going for help was a better idea.

They turned and sprinted together up Main Street. Sam turned off at the Barter, while Caitlin kept running toward The Martha. She had already tried to explain things to her parents over the phone on the way, but they were having a hard time understanding and she finally just hung up. It would all be easier to explain in person. She also planned to get Alexi if he was in his usual place in the library.

Sam jumped up the steps to the theater lobby. He had to tell Ginny and Jake what they'd learned about Nick and how he'd trapped Derek. They both knew him. Maybe they'd be able to talk some sense into the man.

He burst through the doors of the auditorium and sprinted down the side aisle just as Ginny was wheeling Jake toward him in the wheelchair. Fisher walked a few steps behind, but they all stopped in their tracks when they saw Sam.

Fisher glared as he approached. "You kids are like a swarm of pesky gnats, always buzzing around, aren't you?"

Sam stopped and bent over to his knees, panting.

"Don't talk to him like that," said Jake.

Sam tried to speak, but he couldn't catch his breath.

"What's wrong, Sam?" asked Ginny, coming in front of Jake to check on him. "Where are Derek and Caitlin?"

"Derek," gasped Sam. "He's trapped. With Nick."

"Sam, what are you saying?" asked Ginny. "Is Derek in trouble?"

Fisher shook his head. "It's like trying to understand a dog."

Jake growled and pushed his wheelchair backward into Fisher, pinning him against the closest row of seats. "That's quite enough out of you, buddy."

Fisher held up his hands. "All right. You don't have to be so sensitive. Please remove your chair from my foot."

Sam cleared his throat and tried to focus as he stood up straight. "Nick is the one who sent the letters. At least we think so."

"Nick Bulgari?" asked Jake. "Does he still live around here?"

Ginny looked surprised. "Sam, are you sure? That seems unlikely."

"Yes," Sam cried. "And he has Derek trapped. We have to save him."

"Trapped?" said Jake. "Where?"

"At The Tavern. Derek snuck up to his office to look for clues."

Ginny pressed her hand against her forehead as she closed her eyes. "I told you kids to let us handle it."

Fisher chuckled behind them. "The hits just keep coming." He stepped toward the side exit. "I've had quite enough of this sorry production." He stared over at Ginny and Jake. "You know my terms. I'll expect to hear from you."

Sam didn't know what that meant, but he didn't have time to think about Fisher. They were wasting too much time. Maybe Caitlin should have been the one to come to the theater since no one seemed to believe what he was saying.

Ginny shook her head. "I'm sure this must be some kind of misunderstanding."

"Why would Nick want to send me death threats?" asked Jake. "I haven't seen him in twenty years."

Sam quickly tried to explain things. "We saw a picture in the lobby. It said that you were an understudy when Nick was the lead, is that right?"

"That's true," said Jake. "He had an accident…" His voice trailed off as if the pieces were finally coming together in his mind.

Ginny's face flashed a similar recognition. "Oh my gosh. He fell into the Trap Room and broke his leg." She stared at Jake in the wheelchair. "You don't think…"

"Yes!" Sam shouted. "He's the one who hurt Jake. That's what I've been trying to tell you. We have to do something!"

Then the door to the lobby banged open. They all turned and looked up in surprise as Derek and Nick appeared at the back of the theater.

Nick froze when he saw who was standing by the stage. For a second, it looked like he might make a run for it, but then an eerie grin swept over his face. He seemed to embrace the surprise, and he pushed Derek further down the aisle. "Isn't this cozy," he snarled.

"Nick?" said Ginny. "What's going on?"

Jake tried to stand, but grimaced in pain and dropped back into the wheelchair. "It's been a long time, Nick."

Nick pushed Derek into an aisle seat and stepped close to Jake. "Not long enough. How's that leg working out for you?"

"I think it'll heal," Jake replied calmly. "Tell me you had nothing to do with the accident. Whatever feelings you've been holding against me… this is no way to handle it."

A deep howl of laughter reverberated across the theater. "Oh, that's rich. It really is. The mighty Jacob Greensboro wants to talk it out. I've had a long time to think about how you snatched away my dreams. If not for some dumb luck, that should have been me who was plucked out of obscurity and whisked off to Hollywood, not you."

The back door banged open again, and Caitlin and her parents rushed around the corner. Behind them was Alexi, a confused look on his face. Mrs. Murphy hurried down to them. "Boys, are you okay?" When Sam and Derek nodded, she looked to her sister. "Ginny? What's this all about?"

"We're all just discovering that for ourselves, I'm afraid," Ginny answered.

Alexi was a little slower to make it to the stage, but when he got there, he stopped and looked up at his son. His face filled with concern. "Nicholas?"

"This isn't about you, Dad," Nick answered curtly. "Why don't you head back to your precious hotel?"

Alexi wasn't going to leave that easily. "What have you done, my son?"

Nick wouldn't look his father in the eye. "I don't know what you're all talking about."

Sam knew he couldn't wait for Jake to jump up and save the day like he did in his movies. It was up to them. He moved closer to Nick. "Why don't you just admit what you've done? We've pieced the clues together and they all lead to one person. You!"

Ginny still didn't seem ready to accept it. "Kids, let's not accuse him without proof."

Caitlin stepped to Sam's side. "He's right. Nick told us himself that he worked here on stage and in the crew.

He would have known all about how the sets, ropes, and sandbags worked."

Nick shook his head. "That's preposterous. And I suppose, after getting into the theater unseen and cutting some rope, I would have been able to just vanish into thin air with no one seeing me?"

Caitlin nodded. "I couldn't figure that out either, at first. But then I realized you had a perfect escape route. You used the tunnel to sneak away quickly after cutting the rope." She turned to Sam and Derek. "Remember the evidence of recent construction we found down there? It all makes sense now. He must have been clearing the tunnel so he could get from the theater to the hotel without being seen. That's why the doors were unsealed at the other end."

"That's insane," bellowed Nick.

Alexi looked at his son and held up his hands. "I'm afraid it isn't. Nicholas approached me several weeks ago about getting access to the tunnel from the hotel side. He wanted to look at reopening the tunnel. He said it would be good for business."

Sam looked confused. "Why would he ask you about fixing the hotel tunnel? Because you like to sit in the library?"

Nick broke out laughing. "Oh, is that what he told you? That he just likes to sit there and play chess? Trust me, there is little my father cares about more than his precious hotel."

"Wait a minute," said Derek. "*Your* hotel?"

Alexi nodded slowly. "Yes, I don't like to mention it to the guests, but I own The Martha." He looked back hopefully at the kids. "But none of that means my son did anything to Mr. Greensboro. What is your proof?"

Sam tried to think of what else they'd skipped. He knew in his bones that Nick was the culprit. Had everything they'd shared not been enough?

Derek flashed him a knowing glance. "I found the proof. Plenty of it, in fact. He has a stash of magazine and newspaper clippings in his office above The Tavern. They're all about one thing—Jacob Greensboro."

Sam watched Alexi's hopeful expression sink. He felt bad for the old man. No one wants to think that their child has done something terrible. But the facts are the facts.

Sam looked back just as Nick bolted up the aisle. He was making a run for it!

Suddenly Nick stopped in the middle of the aisle. Sam couldn't see why at first, but then it became clear. A police officer walked slowly toward him from the back of the theater. "Evening, Ginny. Which of you folks is parked out front in the Handicap spot without a sticker?" The policeman saw Nick's face and then scanned the group by the stage and seemed to realize something was wrong.

"Don't let that man leave, Officer," Jake shouted confidently in his best Clint Patterson voice.

To his credit, the officer caught on quickly. He stepped down the aisle and pointed to a red velvet seat.

Nick put his hands to his face and collapsed into the chair.

"Okay, who's going to tell me what's going on here?" asked the officer.

Derek jogged up toward him with a smile. "Well, it all started when I got lost at the rest stop on the way from Richmond, Officer."

CHAPTER TWENTY-FIVE

W hen Sam and Derek drove onto Main Street with their parents several months later, it was hard to believe all that had happened since their last visit. They were back in town for a Grand Reopening of the Barter Theatre, and appropriately, it was starting with the show it had ended with—*Red Riding Hood.* The timing of the opening had to do with a lot of things, but mostly Jacob Greensboro's schedule. He was back, starring in the role of the wolf, but he'd also been doing a lot more behind the scenes this time around.

Jake had become an investor in the Barter and a member of the foundation's board of directors. He also took over the ownership stake that Bernard and his Wolf Hills Investments had clawed their way into. Besides his own investment, Jake had also organized a benefit event with all his A-list celebrity friends from Hollywood. It raised a tremendous amount of money for the theater and even pulled in other actors who had their beginnings at the Barter.

Ginny said it was hard to believe how many lives the theater had touched. When people heard the Barter was in trouble, they came from far and wide to lend a hand. Just like the old black and white movie that Sam's mom liked to watch each Christmas, *It's a Wonderful Life*. There was even a truckload of produce dropped off one morning, likely in tribute to the Barter's roots, but Ginny said she sold it all to the local grocery store for a healthy profit.

While it hadn't been the sort of publicity Jake would have chosen, since his accident at the Barter, his career was rebounding. The news of how Nick had attacked him on stage, plus Jake's efforts to save the Barter, really seemed to resonate with people. Since the accident, studios had offered him dozens of potential roles, which he said were light years ahead of what he'd been receiving previously. Rumor even had it that Clint Patterson would soon make another appearance on the big screen.

The Barter wasn't the only part of Abingdon that people loved, of course. Once word spread that Bernard was trying to buy up the historic spots around town to build a corporate retreat conference center and amusement park, there were protests everywhere to stop it. Ginny said that nearly every local resident across three counties had a sign on their front lawn or a sticker on their back bumper calling to save Abingdon's history. When an investigative reporter at the local paper got her hands on the plans for the new complex and published them, it was all over. With the town and surrounding areas in an uproar, Bernard quietly gave up his efforts. Rumor had it that he was moving WHI across the country to try his scheme on the poor folks of another unsuspecting town. No one heard from Fisher again. At least not in Abingdon. He seemed to float in and out with the breeze like an apparition.

In addition to his investment in the theater, Jake gave Ginny a loan. This one had no strings attached, other than a referral to a good accountant to handle the books. While she was free of Fisher's fangs, she still had to face the music with the authorities. Apparently, her taking money from the theater and using it to pay off her own debts was a crime called embezzlement. She faced a serious fine and possible prison time for her poor decisions. Jake and the board were hoping Ginny could still run the theater's creative productions. He and Caitlin's mom had lined up dozens of people from Abingdon and friends of the Barter to speak on Ginny's behalf, but they also knew she had to be accountable for what she'd done. Everyone was hopeful the judge would be lenient since it was her first offense, but it was hard to predict what would happen. Whenever the subject came up, Caitlin got pretty upset, so Sam tried to be as supportive as he could.

As they had learned that surprising night at the Barter, Alexi Bulgari was not just a kindly old man who liked to play chess in The Martha's library. He owned the hotel along with half a dozen other historic properties across the Southeast. He'd made a small fortune in the computer chip industry and then invested most of his money into properties like The Martha. Alexi explained that he'd never truly considered selling the hotel to WHI. He appreciated its history far too much, and Sam came to like the old man much more than he'd originally thought.

His son, unfortunately, was another matter. It seemed Nick had never gotten over the rejection and heartache he'd faced at the Barter. His bitterness over what he viewed as being cheated out of his future by Jacob Greensboro had festered for years, likely sabotaging his efforts in all the different businesses he tried and possibly even his marriage. Instead of being happy for Jake and moving on with his life, he let his jealousy and anger set up shop deep within his heart. When he'd learned Jake was coming back to Abingdon, he'd begun plotting his revenge. Unlike Ginny, Nick didn't have dozens of people lined up to say good things about him, and he was likely going to be in deep trouble when his court date rolled around.

As Sam, Derek, and Caitlin walked up to Main Street along with their parents, it seemed like Hollywood had descended upon the little town of Abingdon. Spotlights and camera crews were lined up outside the Barter, and photographers flashed their cameras at the two families like they were movie stars in their own rights.

Derek was eating up all the attention, posing on the red carpet in a pair of aviator sunglasses. "See, now we really seem like VIPs. It was just a matter of time for word to get out."

Sam wasn't as crazy about the whole ordeal as his brother, feeling more than a little uncomfortable in his shirt and tie. But he supposed it was a small price to pay for getting to be part of such a special night.

This time they sat in the lower section of seats, just a few rows from the Barter's stage. Sam glanced at Caitlin in the seat next to him. She looked pretty in her sparkly blue dress. The crowd hushed as the lights dimmed and Ginny once again walked out to the edge of the stage in front of the curtain.

"Thank you all for coming—" Ginny paused, working hard to keep her emotions in check. "This has been quite a journey for many of us here at the Barter. I can't begin to express how grateful we are for your support. It is so wonderful to be back with you here and introducing the show I know you are all dying to see."

Everyone applauded and Derek made a loud whistle with his fingers. Ginny spoke about the performance and praised all Jake's efforts to raise money for the theater. She spoke about the importance of the arts and how proud Robert Porterfield would be to see the community rally around the Barter. "Thanks to your generosity, the Barter now has an endowment which will allow us to operate for many, many years to come."

Again, the audience roared, some even rising from their seats.

"I'd also like to recognize the particularly daring work

of three young people. Without their efforts, we might not be here for this performance. They're here tonight, so please give a big hand for Sam, Derek, and Caitlin!" Ginny motioned for them to stand, and while it was a little awkward, they all rose from their seats to a big ovation.

"Finally, before we begin our show this evening, I'd like to invite a very special performer to the stage. This is a young woman whose character, resourcefulness, and intelligence continue to inspire me. She also happens to be my niece, so I'm particularly proud. Tonight, we invite her onto the stage to perform an original song she wrote for the guitar. Please welcome for the very first time to the Barter stage, my niece, the incomparable Caitlin Murphy!"

From the way her eyes grew big as saucers, it looked like Caitlin had no clue that her aunt would call her to the stage. She gripped Sam's arm tightly. "Sam, I don't know…"

He chuckled, since it wasn't often that he had to convince Caitlin to do something risky. "Go on, you'll be great." As the audience continued applauding, he nudged her from the seat.

"I don't even have my guitar," she whispered to her parents as she wobbled toward the aisle. Mr. Murphy pointed to Ginny, now holding a guitar up on the stage. "We may have snuck it into the car."

Sam felt like he was at an awards show as Caitlin walked up the stairs and then across the stage. Despite the surprise, she'd been practicing her guitar and writing songs for months. If she could get over her nerves, he was confident that she'd do great.

Caitlin gave her aunt a big hug and took the guitar. She moved over to a stool and a microphone that had been placed in the center of the stage and stared out at the audience through the lights.

"Hi, everybody," she called shyly. "Thanks for coming out to support this great old theater." There was more applause, and Derek yelled, "Go, Caitlin!" obnoxiously.

She blushed, but then adjusted the microphone and placed her fingers against the guitar strings. "Um, this is a song I wrote. It's called, 'Goodnight, Daniel Boone.'"

The crowd grew silent as Caitlin softly strummed a couple of chords and then started singing.

Late at night up in those Abingdon hills
All the wolves and the ponies run free
No cars or trains chugging over the ridge
Just forests clear to the sea

Before the town and crowds were here
Looking for a real good show
People brought crops straight out of the ground
Payin' only with things they could grow

What did you dream about, Daniel Boone?
Camping out under the stars
Searching for a path over the ridge

Knowing it might be so far

What did it feel like, Daniel Boone?
Alone out there on the trail
Listening to the wolves and the coyotes sing
Till morning with its light so pale

Did you explore where the hikers now roam
Chasing white blazes through the trees
Could you have walked the train track route
Where smoke would darken the breeze

What would you make of our hi-tech world
We're still all figuring things out
So many changes since you walked these woods
As a young pioneer scout

What did you dream about, Daniel Boone?
Camping out under the stars
Searching for a path over the ridge
Knowing that it might be far

What did it feel like, Daniel Boone?
Alone out there on the trail
Listening to the wolves and the coyotes sing
Till morning with its light so pale

I've got a brand-new story to tell
Staring at the same full moon

I really hope my show goes well
Goodnight, Daniel Boone

When Caitlin finished her song, it was hard for Sam to even remember that they'd come for the play. Watching her sing softly along to her guitar, it felt like someone had sprinkled magic dust over all their heads.

When she strummed the last chord, the place erupted in applause. The smile that spread across Caitlin's face was so big it seemed like it could reach the whole way up the Creeper Trail. Maybe even back to Richmond.

As he stood and clapped, Sam glanced behind him to the balcony. Maybe it was the lights, or perhaps just more of the magic dust, but he caught another glimpse of the man in the white three-piece suit waving down to the stage in appreciation. Sam nudged Derek and pointed to the spot in the balcony, but when he looked back, Porterfield was gone. Had he even been there in the first place? It was hard to tell.

When the applause died down, Caitlin made her way back to her seat. She grinned at him like she couldn't believe what had just happened. Sam didn't know what more he could say, so he just winked.

Then the lights dimmed, the curtain parted into the wings, and he settled back and prepared to be captivated.

Let the show begin.

ACKNOWLEDGMENTS

Virginia is a big place, and while it's not approaching the size of a Texas or California, its distinct regions are filled with history. One of the areas I hadn't yet written about was the rural southwest, so it was fun to research and explore near Roanoke, Wytheville, Abingdon, Damascus, and Bristol. I originally got the idea when visiting Greendale Elementary in Abingdon in 2019 when students made art projects with suggestions of where would make a great future VA Mystery. Several mentioned The Martha Washington Inn, and as I researched further, I discovered the town was full of interesting history, from being coined *Wolf Hills* by Daniel Boone, The Creeper Trail, The Tavern, intersecting with the Appalachian Trail, and of course the Barter Theatre.

Special thanks goes to Jacqueline Blevins at the Barter Theatre who generously provided her time to meet my family at The Martha, a Barter backstage tour, and provide a wealth of insights. We also enjoyed a performance of *9 to 5* on the Barter Stage. We enjoyed renting bikes from Sun Dog Outfitter in Damascus for a ride down The Virginia Creeper Trail and the very informative shuttle driver. Thank you to Brenda Sprinkle and the students of Greendale Elementary for pointing me toward writing about Abingdon several years ago.

Some of the books that were helpful in my research included *Daniel Boone* by John Mack Faragher, *Blood and Treasure: Daniel Boone and the Fight for America's First Frontier* by Bob Drury and Tom Clavin, and my favorite book about The Appalachian Trail which I've read several times, *A Walk in the Woods*, by Bill Bryson.

My only time on stage for a theatrical production was in middle school, performing in a collection of small roles as a Fireman, the Engineer, and even an unfortunate man locked in a coffin! Each time I hear *Burning Down the House* by Talking Heads, it reminds me of the curtain call at the end of those shows.

May, 2023 will be the ten-year anniversary of the first Virginia Mysteries book, *Summer of the Woods*. So many people have been critical in bringing these books to readers. I couldn't do any of this without the love and support of my family, so thank you to Mary, Matthew, Josh, and Aaron. I rely on a top-notch publishing team—Dane at eBook Launch who continues to amaze me with his cover illustrations, Kim Sheard and Stephanie Parent for their edits, and series audiobook narrator, Tom McElroy.

Thank you to the thousands of students, parents, teachers, librarians, booksellers, and readers of all ages who've supported my writing. It means so much.

ABOUT THE AUTHOR

Steven K. Smith is the author of *The Virginia Mysteries*, *Brother Wars*, and *Final Kingdom* series for middle grade readers. He lives with his wife, three sons, and a golden retriever in Richmond, Virginia.

For more information, visit:

www.stevenksmith.net

Email: steve@myboys3.com

Facebook & Instagram: @stevenksmithauthor

Twitter: @stevenksmith1

ALSO BY STEVEN K. SMITH

The Virginia Mysteries:

Summer of the Woods
Mystery on Church Hill
Ghosts of Belle Isle
Secret of the Staircase
Midnight at the Mansion
Shadows at Jamestown
Spies at Mount Vernon
Escape from Monticello
Pictures at the Protest
Pirates on the Bay
Danger on the Stage

Brother Wars Series:

Brother Wars
Cabin Eleven
The Big Apple

Final Kingdom Trilogy (Ages 10+)

The Missing
The Recruit
The Bridge

CHAT

Sam, Derek, and Caitlin aren't the only kids who crave adventure. Whether near woods in the country or amidst tall buildings and the busy urban streets of a city, every child needs exciting ways to explore his or her imagination, excel at learning and have fun.

A portion of the proceeds from *The Virginia Mysteries* series will be donated to the great work of **CHAT (Church Hill Activities & Tutoring)**. CHAT is a nonprofit group that works with kids in the Church Hill neighborhood of inner-city Richmond, Virginia.

To learn more about CHAT, including opportunities to volunteer or contribute financially, visit **www.chatrichmond.org.**

DID YOU ENJOY DANGER ON THE STAGE?

WOULD YOU ... REVIEW?

Online reviews are crucial for indie authors like me. They help bring credibility and make books more discoverable by new readers. No matter where you purchased your book, if you could take a few moments and give an honest review at **Amazon** or **Goodreads**, I'd be grateful.

If you're a teacher, be sure to check out the reading comprehension quiz, class and school ordering discounts, historical links, and other materials on my website at stevenksmith.net.

Manufactured by Amazon.ca
Acheson, AB

13817939R00132